Carson H

Search

Carson Hill Ranch Series: Book 2

Amelia Rose

Dedication

To YOU, The reader.

Thank you for your support.

Thank you for your emails.

Thank you for your reviews.

Thank you for reading and joining me on this road.

Copyright

Contents

Carson Hill Ranch Series

Chapter One

Carey stared wistfully in the distance, watching as the truck containing the happy bride and groom left a trail of dust in its wake. As the couple sped off toward their honeymoon, he couldn't help but feel out of sorts and alone in a way he'd never experienced. Of course, he was happy for his brother, Casey, and his new bride, Miranda, but Carey had never really been apart from his twin brother. Something told him this was only the beginning of how things were about to change, not only between the two brothers but also within the family as a whole.

They'd been a close-knit family for as long as Carey could remember, probably brought even closer from losing their mother at such a young age. For Casey and Carey, the oldest of the Carson boys, all the way down to the fifteen-year-old twins, Seamus and Jacob, with middle brothers, Joseph and Anders, in between, being a part of their ranching family meant they were always together, always looking out for each other, and working toward a common goal for the family.

But that was about to change. Shouts of, "You're next, Carey Carson!" had sounded around him as he walked through the different patches of people working on the drive, and it tore him in two. On the one hand, finding someone who was practically a stranger on the Internet like Casey had—with way too much help from his or her meddling but well-intentioned father—just wasn't for him but neither was sitting out here on a desolate ranch and hoping a beautiful girl just fell from the sky.

Ever since Dad had gotten a wild hair about finding the brothers romance and set up online dating profiles for both Casey and Carey, they had been on edge. It had only taken a matter of weeks for someone to answer Dad's ad for Casey but luckily, it seemed to work out. Carey wasn't so sure lightning would strike twice so unless he wanted Dad to play matchmaker with

6

strangers on cowboy dating sites, he'd better convince the old man that one wedding around here was enough for a while.

And with the cattle drive going on and the vacationing wannabe cowboys to look after, at least there wouldn't be any chance to think about some girl showing up on the doorstep the way Miranda had, towing her kid sister, Gracie, with her. Speaking of Gracie…

"Where are you off to, kiddo?" Carey called out, spying thirteen-year-old Gracie riding her mare away from the group and toward a small cluster of cowboys from the Carson ranch.

"I can't take it anymore, Carey! It's only been a day and a half, and already those city people are driving me crazy!" She grabbed the sides of her head, managing to toss her hat back and letting it hang by its leather chord.

"If I remember correctly, weren't you one of those city people not too long ago?" Carey teased, pointing out that Gracie had only been on the ranch a short time, and that this was her first cattle drive.

"But they're loud and they're rude! They keep wanting to know if we have Wi-Fi…this is a freakin' cattle drive! What do they need with Wi-Fi, anyway? We're on a cattle drive!" she cried. "Please give me a different job. I don't care if it's picking up the poop all the way to Missouri and back, please! Anything but hanging out with the city people!"

"I dunno, kid. That was the job Dad gave you, so it's kind of out of my hands. Of course, that was before your sister knew we were getting her hitched and sending her home," he said with a smile, referring to the surprise wedding they'd staged without her knowing. Miranda had thought she was out here for the cattle drive and to help look after the people who paid to join the ranchers on the trip, but they sprung it on her at the last minute that she and Casey were getting married and heading off to their honeymoon instead of driving oversized, smelly cattle. "I'll check with him and see if you can help with the feeding, or something like that."

"Thank you, Carey!" Gracie squealed, throwing her arms around his neck and giving him an awkward hug from where she still sat in the saddle. She gave a light tug to her reins and nudged her horse with the heel of her boot, leading it off in the direction of some of the other ranchers. Carey watched her go, wondering how he'd found himself in charge of taking care of a kid on this event. *The things a best man will do for his twin, the groom,* Carey thought as he shook his head and returned to his tasks.

"Hey, Carey," Bernard Carson called out to his son. "we need you over here a second." Carey strode toward his elderly father—some fifty years older than his first-born sons, thanks to marrying late in life himself—and smiled at the old man.

"Yeah, Dad? What's up?" he asked, taking off his hat and wiping at his brow with the back of his hand, fanning himself with the hat for a moment before placing it back over his sweat-curled, shaggy brown hair.

"Well, with your brother gone for the rest of the drive, we'll need to arrange for someone to drive the truck. I was hoping you could switch off every third day, so that no one person has to keep doing it. I didn't mind making Casey do it so much because he'd been injured only last week, but I hate to stick someone in the cab of the truck too long and make them miss out, especially if they're able-bodied enough to get to ride with the group. What do you think?"

"Sure, Dad, that sounds fair. I'll be glad to take my turn, rather than stick some poor hired hand with having to do it for the whole time. Who else ya have so far?" Together, father and son poured over the notes on Bernard's clipboard, crossing out some information, adding other names to the list. The sun beat down from overhead as they worked through their final plans, the ranchers and hired helpers moving the cattle into position around them.

Later in the day, when the group stopped to water the cattle and have a meal, Joseph had a chance to pull Carey aside. "I can't believe Casey actually went through with it," he started, stirring his fork absentmindedly around on his tin plate.

"Went through with what? Getting married? Why not? Miranda seems like a great girl. I mean, she'd have to be, not to run screaming away from the bunch of us." He nudged his younger brother jokingly with his shoulder.

"Oh, no. I didn't mean Miranda. She seems really incredible," Joseph interrupted, realizing how his words could be taken. "I don't know, the whole thing just seemed so weird. I mean, come on. Who meets a stranger on the Internet and gets married? It's a little creepy, don't you think?"

Carey looked out over the resting herd and the workers standing at ease in a wide formation around the group. He'd grown up with these very ranch hands, most of whom actually lived on the Carson Hill Ranch because of its distance from the nearest town. Carey and his five brothers had even gone to school on the ranch, along with a handful of other kids whose families lived on the 800,000-acre property year-round.

"Well, when you put it that way, it is kind of weird, I suppose, but how else was Casey supposed to find a wife?" he asked his younger brother. "This isn't exactly a hotbed of social activity out where we are, and the days of placing a newspaper ad for a wife are kind of over."

"Right. So, is that what you're gonna do? Click a few buttons on a computer and order a wife instead? Maybe have her shipped overnight delivery?" Joseph teased. Carey knew his brother was only kidding, but that thought had bothered him, too. Now that his dad had successfully married off one of his sons with his crazy plan of creating dating profiles behind their backs and pretending to be the twins for the purposes of emailing back, it could mean he'd be on the warpath to repeat his success.

"No, I don't think so. It sure worked out well enough for Casey, but what if he just got lucky? I just can't see myself talking to some girl through a computer screen and thinking that means true love," Carey conceded, going back to paying full attention to his dinner plate. "Guess I'll have to go looking for a girl the old-fashioned way."

"Oh, that's nice. You mean the local whorehouse?" Joseph asked with a wide-eyed, innocent expression that hid the semi-cruel sense of humor underneath.

"You watch your mouth," Carey cautioned in a sterner voice, shoving his brother painfully in the shoulder with both hands. Joseph must have forgotten that only days ago, two runaways had shown up on the ranch, having escaped from one of the worst offenders in the town. At that very moment, they were holed up in an outbuilding some 200 acres from the main house of Carson Hill, suffering through the pains of withdrawal.

"Oh, crap," Joseph said, recognizing from Carey's expression what he'd just implied. "I wasn't thinking about them. You have to believe me, Carey, I was only kidding. I was just running my stupid mouth."

"It's okay, but you have to be more careful. What if that kind of talk got back to those poor girls? I'm not stupid and I'm not a completely inexperienced kid…I know some of these guys have already met with those girls once or twice before, if not more often. You can't go talking about them like that, especially with these guys around."

"I know! I said I was sorry, I really am," the younger brother continued, a look of guilt crossing his face.

"It's all right. I know you didn't mean anything. Just be more careful. Come on, let's finish up. It looks like we're ready to move out." Carey and Joseph joined the line of ranchers and vacationers who brought their lunch dishes back to the rolling kitchen truck before heading back to their assigned positions within the drive. Although a modern cattle drive hardly even looked like what the cowboys of the Old West endured, what with retrofitted kitchens on wheels doing all the cooking, a medical truck providing support, and even an extra vehicle or two meeting the group at different points along the way in case anyone needed anything, Bernard did his best to keep some of that original spirit alive. That's why every year, people paid good money to join the drive, "city people", who spent a week or two with the group just to get away from their busy lives and smartphones for a little while. Helping move thirty or forty thousand cows from one state to another may not have been as glamorous as a trip to the Caribbean or a ski vacation but people still signed up, year after year, hoping to get away from it all and carve out just a small portion of peace and quiet while still being a part of something big.

This drive was no different. If Carey bothered to look hard enough, he could have started to pick out some of the differences among their guests, but who was he kidding? They were all the same, at least on the surface. They all had lives and jobs that didn't involve ranching or working the land, and they all had money to burn to pretend like they wanted to live like this. He knew from experience that every one of them would be hopping on the plane in a few days, eager to get back to the land of modern plumbing and central heating. There wasn't much point in learning anything more than their first names, and even that information was only useful for calling out to one of them if they were about to do something dumb.

Carey swung up in the saddle and steered his horse to the lead team, ready to swap out with anyone who might need a break for

11

a little while. Leading was stressful, especially because the rest of society didn't care too much for the old ways. Lead riders had to watch out for all kinds of dangers like speeding cars and eighteen-wheelers and alert the rest of the group, so there was no daydreaming up front.

"Hey, Jeff, I'll come on up here for a while if anyone wants to take a rest along the sides of the pack," Carey offered, coming up close to one of the professional drovers, who was hired every year just for the duration of events like this one.

"Yeah, right," Jeff said with a pleasant laugh. "You just want to get away from those city people. You're not fooling anyone with this 'I'm here to help' act you're putting on!"

"I'm telling you, Jeff. I don't know if I can take it anymore!" Carey laughed along quietly, looking around to make sure no one overheard them. "I've put up with these yahoos every year, and even after I think I've heard it all, somehow, the next crop has someone even worse. Remember that guy who brought his own gun on the trip and was mad when Dad made him leave it locked in the safe? Like we were going to need to deputize him and ride out with a posse against Black Bart to save Miss Polly from the train tracks, or something." Jeff laughed at Carey's description, slapping his thigh with his reins as he roared. "This time, we have two girls who have no business out here, one who's scared of every little shadow and one who thinks all men were put on this planet for her to hate."

"Oh, sounds like you're already getting along great with the ladies, huh?" Jeff joked, pointing out that Carey's twin had just gotten married, leaving plenty of room for him to find a girl of his own.

"Don't start on me. I can already feel Dad breathing down my neck. Not that I would ever wish Casey or Miranda anything but the best but deep down, I was kind of hoping Dad would realize he should have stayed out of it if they didn't patch things up like

12

they did. Now that he's tasted matchmaking success, it's like I can feel his eyes on me, like he has a giant bull's eye on my back for his Cupid's arrow."

"Yeah, I wish I had something helpful to say there, buddy, but I'm sure you're right. He's gonna be on you to get married next!" Jeff grinned as he spoke, obviously not anywhere near as sympathetic as his words should have been. They rode along in silence for a few more minutes, one smiling in triumph, the other hanging his head. "You know, there is one thing you can do. The only way to head off your dad's ideas of romance is to beat him to the punch."

"What do you mean?" Carey asked, hope coloring his voice.

"Well, find your own girl without his help. Maybe then he'll leave you alone. Your only other option is to hope that Casey and Miranda start a family right away. Maybe having some grandkids running around the place will give your dad something to focus on rather than playing love triangle with your future all day."

"That's great. Fat lot of good you did in the hope department!" Carey called out as he rode away, mentally preparing himself to rejoin the group of city people who were helping out with various tasks along the route. He took a deep breath, released it, and painted a smile on his face, ready to face them.

Chapter Two

"Karen, can you wait for me? I can't seem to get this dumb horse to want to cooperate," Amy called out as she watched the other woman's retreating back moving farther and farther away. She couldn't be sure, but she thought she heard Karen let out an exasperated sigh, but the other woman did expertly lead her horse back around and come back toward Amy.

"That's because you're not letting him know that you're in charge," Karen said roughly. "You don't have to be cruel, but let him know who's boss or he'll walk all over you." Karen snatched the reins out of Amy's hands and made a sharp clucking noise to the brown, doe-eyed animal, pulling it forward.

"Don't hurt him!" Amy cried, grasping the saddle with both hands to keep from falling as the large horse lurched forward.

"I'm not hurting him," Karen argued. "but you have to give him instructions. He doesn't want to stand there looking like an idiot any more than you do, and if you're not going to tell him where to go in the only way he understands, he can't move. Now, move, horse!" She tossed the reins back to Amy, more than a little disgusted by the younger woman's innate air of weakness. *If this drive did nothing more than teach her to grow a backbone*, Karen thought harshly. *It would have been money well spent.*

Amy dropped her face as shame crept up and washed over her, letting her strawberry blonde curls fall in waves over her face. She was always letting other people boss her around, and it had landed her into one failed relationship or friendship after another: work friends, boyfriends, bosses, even professors in school now that she'd gone back to college to work on her graduate degree. It hadn't always been like this but lately, she'd begun tolerating it when people effortlessly walked all over her, and she knew it was because she let them. She just didn't know how to stand up for herself. *At least the horse isn't walking all over me*, she thought. But she knew that was only because he wasn't walking much at all.

"Hey now," Carey said, riding up alongside Amy and ducking his head to see her face under the wide brim of her hat. "Why the long face?"

"It's nothing…" she began, looking away and blinking back the threat of tears.

"I was talking to the horse," Carey answered. Amy looked up at him, crestfallen, until he smiled disarmingly. "That was a joke. Get it? You know, the old joke? 'Why the long face?'" Amy laughed half-heartedly in spite of herself and shook her head. "Never mind. No, I really was talking to you. What's wrong? You don't seem to be having a lot of fun out here."

"I guess I'm just not a natural born horseman. Horsewoman. Cowboy. Oh, whatever." Amy looked self-consciously at the others from their group, who were planted at various points along the ranks of cattle. Everyone seemed to be engaged in what they were doing, maybe not all of them smiling and laughing as they worked, but at least determined-looking and taking an active part in the drive.

"Well, I heard your friend over there, and she's only partly right. You don't have to go attacking the horse, but you do have to tell him what to do. Think of it this way, he really wants to do what you want him to, but no one told him what you want. He doesn't speak your language. What would you do if I walked up to you and rattled off a bunch of stuff in Chinese? You'd just stand there, looking confused. I could shove you and kick you and make you move, I could even shout at you in Chinese, but you still wouldn't know what I wanted. Here."

Carey reached across Amy and took the reins from her hands, causing her pulse to beat that much faster at being so close to someone as rugged and drop-dead gorgeous as Carey. He flicked the reins lightly so that the hanging loop gently slapped against the horse's front shoulder while nudging the animal's rear shoulder with the toe of his boot. Amy looked relieved when the horse began to walk purposefully, not rearing or taking off, but moving with purpose along with the rest of the group.

"See there? That's his language. I just told him to go forward and step with his right leg first. The problem is a sudden jerk of his reins will tell him that there's a danger ahead but if he doesn't see any danger, he's going to be really confused by why you're acting crazy. Just give your instructions gently but firmly."

"I just don't want to hurt him," Amy said quietly, scratching at the horse's neck in front of her saddle.

"But now you're confusing him," Carey laughed. "You told him to move forward, but then you told him to stand still so you could scratch him! Which one do you think he's going to do, walk or be petted?" Carey smiled at Amy, understanding that she was so far out of her element that he couldn't assume she knew what he meant. "He knows you like him, and you can pet him all you want when you're done working. Remember, these aren't our pets. Even though we care for them and make sure they're as happy as they can be, they're still working members of the ranch, just like all of us cowboys. No one's coming up behind me and giving me a back rub when I'm out here!"

I'd like to, Amy thought, causing a sudden blush to shine through the fair skin of her cheeks and surprising herself with the brazen thought. *I could do more than that, too.*

Carey couldn't help but notice her embarrassment and didn't let himself even wonder what thought she'd had that caused it. He nodded awkwardly and tipped his hat, then rode back toward the front to check on the others. He looked back once or twice to make sure she was still doing okay, and was taken aback when he caught her looking at him one time.

"How's the babysitting going?" a ranch hand said under his breath when Carey began to pass around him.

"I think it's okay," he answered, looking over the new people and counting them to make sure they were all still with the group. "No one too obnoxious or too incompetent, I'm just worried about a couple of them who obviously haven't been on a horse before."

"Hey, if it's any help at all, there's a couple of 'em back there who can ride right up here with me," the hand said slyly, patting the saddle in front of him. "Wouldn't mind having to see a few of their faces more closely for the rest of the trip! I mean, only if it helps *you*, of course!."

"You say that now," Carey said with a quiet laugh. "There's one or two in that group who would rip your chest open with their claws and feast on your beating heart!" The hand, David, laughed so loudly, he startled a nearby steer.

"Yeah, I'm pretty sure I met that one already. She took offense when I called her 'ma'am', then told me not to single her out by 'labeling her with her imposed gender identity.' I'm not exactly sure what that means, but I think it's just safer if I don't address her ever again!"

"Just don't make eye contact or speak in her presence, and for the love of Pete, don't look at her chest. I don't want to have to scrape up pieces of you from here to Missouri!" Carey slapped David on the shoulder then continued on.

Chapter Three

By the time lunch rolled around, Bernard had assembled his remaining Carson sons—Carey, Joseph, Seamus, and Jacob—and the two foremen who still worked for the ranch. As much as Bernard hated to admit it, this particular drive had gone so much more smoothly—even with Casey's absence as the oldest son—and the only thing he could attribute it to was the loss of Jack, a longtime foreman for Carson Hill. He wondered, once again, if he'd given the foreman far too much leeway over the two decades Jack had worked for him, especially considering he was crazy enough to murder someone and was now sitting in the state prison, hopefully rotting. The whole thing had made Bernard wonder how much he really knew any of the thirty or forty outsiders who lived on his ranch and worked with his family, day after day.

The faces of his small crew looked up at him from their seats around the table in the large bus-like RV that served as his office during the drive. There were sleeping bunks and a shower that various members of the group could take turns using, and a real bathroom for any one of the paying visitors who was too squeamish to use the facilities the great outdoors had to offer.

Maps were spread on the table in front of them, with marked waypoints as to where they would stop each day. The only thing different about this meeting compared to the same meetings that took place during round ups from a hundred years ago was the presence of iPads, handheld GPS devices, Bernard's laptop, and a few more 21st century items that helped guarantee the drive went off with as little disruption and risk as possible. A satellite phone stood up on the table and its green power LED shone, connecting the middle son, Anders, to the meeting from his place back home in the ranch office.

"I don't see any reason why we can't just add two or three miles a day to the trip and cut out a whole day of the drive," one of the foreman, Dwayne, argued again, pointing to the different spots past each waypoint that would still have plenty of water and access for the vehicles to meet up with the group. "We've never had weather this good, and we're making really great time. We can press on and pick up the pace now."

Even though they were twins, Casey had always held the unofficial position as the oldest Carson boy, the oldest brother, and by rights, that made him more of Bernard's second-in-command. So when everyone looked at Carey, he fought the urge to look over his shoulder for Casey. When he realized that his brother's absence meant he was now a louder voice in the decisions that had to be made, it was both exciting and a little bit unnerving as everyone looked at him for input.

"Well," he began, clearing his throat. "If we walk the cattle more than thirty miles a day, we're going to have some awfully skinny cows to sell when we finally arrive in Missouri. These are animals whose whole lives have been spent just standing around, eating grass all day. If we push 'em too hard, we're liable to lose a lot of their numbers.

"Plus, we have the city people to think about. They paid to come out here for a full drive, and we provided a detailed itinerary so that they could check in with family and friends back home at each of the designated spots. They even get to take that day trip once we reach the state line, remember?"

"Is this a vacation, or a cattle drive?" Dwayne demanded, a tone of disgust creeping into his voice. Bernard watched Carey's face silently to see how he would handle both the second-guessing and the mild impertinence from one of their employees.

"It's both," Carey said in a stern, level voice, looking Dwayne directly in the eye.

"Our ranch's income comes from the sale of the cattle, but also from the tourists who come along each time. We have an obligation to get those cows there in one piece and in good shape, but we also owe it to the people who sent in their checks to take part in it. If we didn't want those people along on 'vacation', then we shouldn't have invited them." Carey let his words sink in and paused to let Dwayne remember that he was talking to one of the future owners of Carson Hill Ranch. Then, he relaxed his expression and lowered his voice to a conversational tone.

"We can't go changing it up now, not when they've paid good money to take part in this drive. We're just gonna have to leave the plans like they are, and count our blessings that the weather has cooperated enough to give us a nice leisurely walk. Besides, it'll give us some extra cushion in case we have any delays and do have to speed up later on."

Everyone nodded in agreement, even Dwayne, and the fluttering feeling in the pit of Carey's stomach died down some. He'd never been the one to speak out and help make the decisions, because he'd always been happy to let Casey take the lead and to support whatever his brother thought up. Now, he sensed the very real loss of his twin and felt alone for the first time since Carey drove away with Miranda. It stung to suddenly find himself out on his own a little, and he couldn't wait for this drive to be over and to head back to the ranch, where they could all be the Carson boys again.

The meeting broke up and the small group descended the steps of the RV to join the other hands and cowboys as they ate their lunch. After getting his plate from the kitchen truck, still affectionately called the chuck wagon as a throwback to the olden days, Carey looked around for a spot to sit down and eat. His attention was pulled to the loud voices of an argument that had broken out among the city people. Walking that way quickly, he caught enough of the conversation to piece together that someone had gone and offended the feminist…again.

"Hi, folks!" Carey called out affectionately, ignoring the ugly looks passing between some of the group members and the irritated glare Karen shot in his direction. He couldn't help but notice that Amy had her head down, looking at the untouched plate in her lap. He dropped down on the grass right beside her with his plate and asked, "Mind if I join you guys? I'm starved!"

Most of them mumbled their agreement and went back to their food and out of the corner of his eye, Carey saw Amy look at him and smile sheepishly. Carey leaned very close to her, so close that she could smell the scent of soap and sunscreen off his skin, and whispered, "What did I miss?"

Amy shrugged, then looked around nervously before answering. "Apparently, 'cowboy' is an ugly word to my people."

He narrowed his eyes in confusion before asking for clarity. "Your people?"

"Girl people. I think we're not supposed to tolerate anyone calling us 'cowboys' but then, it turns out that 'cowgirls' is also off-limits after Bob over there was nice enough to suggest that everyone politely use that word instead."

"What does Karen want everyone to call you then?" Carey said, trying desperately not to laugh, especially once he spied Karen fuming when she noticed Amy talking to him. Of all the stupid arguments for people to have, this one had to be somewhere near the top of the list.

Amy shrugged again. "Cow people? I think? I was trying really hard not to pay attention, but you know how she is."

"Cow people."

"Yup." Amy took a forkful of food and chewed thoughtfully as she remembered the argument over labels, then swallowed before adding, "I might have my terminology wrong, but that's what I suggested just to keep the peace."

"Do you really want to be called a 'cow people'? Because I can totally be respectful to everyone, but even I'm gonna have a hard time remembering to call you cow people."

"What about cow humans?" she suggested in a hushed voice, giving Carey an uncharacteristically conspiratorial grin.

"Now *that* I can do. I can really get behind not labeling people, so we'll go with 'cow humans.'" Carey slid one of the extra cookies off his plate onto her plate as he talked, gesturing with his fork that she needed to eat up now that the sexism ruckus had died down. "So, have you learned to speak horse yet?"

"Fluently, as a matter of fact. My horse and I were actually just having a lovely discussion just this morning on which he thinks will win the next election. Turns out, my horse is voting independent."

"Well, that explains about sixty percent of the problem you've been having with your horse," he replied knowingly.

"What, you don't like his political views?" she demanded with mock anger.

"No, I meant because your horse is a girl, not a boy. I can't speak for everyone, but the gender is usually the first thing most people can tell about a horse, if you know what I mean." He chuckled to himself, then actually laughing out loud when he caught Amy's bemused expression.

"Well, maybe I'm not that kind of girl," she said, turning her head nonchalantly and feigning indifference. "I don't go around peeking between farm animals' legs, I'll have you know. I was raised better than that." The conversation proved to be too hilarious. She couldn't maintain her straight face any longer, and quickly fell victim to a fit of giggles.

Carey laughed loudly, surprised by Amy's sense of humor. She blushed again at the attention and cast a sideways glance at Karen's disgusted look. He noticed the sudden enmity between the two women and asked about it. "Is your friend over there upset? You two arguing?"

"Oh, she's not my friend, not really," Amy answered softly, turning more toward Carey's direction to keep their conversation private. "I only met her on the bus from the airport, and I just kind of latched onto her. She seems to know what she's doing, so I just kind of tagged along. She's very…"

"…Bossy? Cranky? Mean? Bitchy? Murdery?" Carey suggested.

"…Intense. And I don't think 'murdery' is a real word."

"Neither is 'cow people,' but that hasn't stopped anyone. Oh, you have to finish eating, looks like we're heading out soon. Thanks for letting me have lunch with you," Carey said, before scraping the rest of his food up with his spoon.

"No problem. It was nice to have a calm, quiet conversation during a meal for once." Amy smiled when Carey stood and offered her his hand, holding her steady and helping her up. He turned to offer his hand to Karen as well, but pulled his arm back as though she would bite when she looked at him with contempt and stood up on her own.

"Well, I'm open for quiet conversation at every meal. I'll be sure to look for you at dinner. I'll just have to follow the sounds of rabid snarling," Carey promised as bent closer to Amy's ear, jerking his head slightly toward where Karen stood behind him.

"Sounds great," Amy said, smiling at him genuinely as he took her plate and stacked it with his own, then watched him walk back to the chuck wagon to return them. He gave her a small wave before heading off to where his horse was tethered.

"I didn't realize you'd signed up for a single's cruise," Karen said snidely as she passed. "I thought you were here to learn a little bit about being your own woman and taking care of yourself."

Amy sighed and squared her shoulders before turning to face Karen. "I'm here to learn to make my own decisions, too, not to let other people dictate how I should behave. If I happen to have a seat beside someone while I eat, who treats me respectfully and with basic human manners, then that is no one else's concern." She tossed her curly hair over her shoulder and slapped her hat back on her head, marching confidently to follow the rest of the group to their horses.

What am I doing? Amy thought, shocked. *I've never spoken to anyone like that before! My mother would have a fit if she'd heard me be so rude!* And it was true. Only a week ago, Karen's remark would have sent Amy to an empty stall in the nearest ladies' room, ready to dissolve in a snot-filled puddle of tears. Now, Amy dared her to criticize her again, her previous life and her mother be damned. No one was going to talk down to her, but that didn't mean she had to turn into a witch like Karen to stand her ground. Maybe there was something to what she'd heard about these confidence-building trips...and to what she'd always heard about good-looking cowboys.

Karen watched her go, shaking her head in frustration at the way some women threw themselves at the nearest available human with a penis. But this was one time she wasn't going to sit by and watch while some man took advantage of a clueless women who was only using half a brain. She stomped off after Carey, ready to give him a piece of her mind, and Amy's mind, too, for that matter, as the girl clearly wasn't able to do it herself.

Chapter Four

Unfortunately, no one told her horse that Amy had decided to become a new woman who wasn't taking crap from people anymore. The animal was just as stubborn as before, even though she tried to speak to him soothingly while still being firm. It was almost as if the animal could smell and respond to Amy's nervousness, as though being unsure of herself around the oversized creature was a tangible scent.

After taking a deep breath, she hoisted her booted foot up into the stirrup to lift herself into the saddle, only every time she started to put her weight on that leg, the horse would take one step forward. Amy would drop her weight back down on her standing leg in defeat, her boot still in her stirrup, and the horse would hold still once again.

But as soon as she took her weight off the ground and tried pulling herself up into the saddle, the stupid thing would walk again, moving forward and out from under Amy's much-needed leverage. She spoke to the horse calmly and reassuringly but every time she inched off the ground, the dumb beast would take a step.

I went to college, you stupid horse! You're not outsmarting me, she thought angrily, seething to herself in frustration. Moving hopefully too fast for the horse to notice, Amy took a leap as she pulled herself up, aiming herself forward this time so she would move with the horse. Feeling the shift in her weight, the animal stepped backward instead, throwing Amy off balance. When she tried putting her foot back on the ground, the level surface wasn't where she thought it should be, causing her to lose her footing. In its confusion, the horse took off running, dragging Amy along by the foot that was still trapped and twisted within the stirrup.

"No! STOP!" Amy screamed, scrambling to reach for something to pull herself up but resorting, instead, to putting her arms over her face and head to protect them from the horse's stomping hooves. The hard ground scratched painfully through the thin fabric of her shirt, and each rock seemed to embed itself deep in her muscles as she continued to be pulled along. "Someone, help!"

Carey heard Amy's unmistakable voice as she called out in pain, and seeing her horse dragging her toward the herd, his heart nearly stopped. A stampeding horse in the middle of thousands of several-ton cows would get her killed for sure. He steered his horse in her direction and slapped at its neck with the hanging end of his leather reins, urging it on. Coming at her horse from the side, he let go of the reins and leaned toward it, grabbing hold of her reins and simultaneously catching one of her hands as he leaned dangerously close to the ground from where he sat in the saddle.

He sat upright and pulled Amy with him, throwing her in front of him on the saddle. The horses began to slow under Carey's level-headed direction and, together, they worked her foot out of its snare. Amy's horse began to mosey off as though the beast hadn't just nearly killed its would-be rider, while Carey's horse waited patiently for further instructions from its rider.

Carey held Amy in front of him tenderly, afraid to touch her back for fear that anything was torn or broken. She gave way to shaking now that she was safe and could process what happened. She looked up at Carey, willing herself not to cry, to be strong. He watched her face silently, struggling to process what exactly he had felt as he saw her pulled away. Was it fear for her? Of course, just like he would have felt for any member of the group being dragged into harm's way. But it was something else, too, a feeling that he hadn't done enough to protect her, that he was responsible for keeping her safe.

Of course I'm responsible for her, he tried to chastise himself. *I'm a member of this ranch and she's a paying customer.* But he knew that wasn't all that was behind it. It was more like he wanted to protect her…from everything.

"Are you okay?" he asked tentatively, watching her face for her reaction. She nodded quietly, too afraid to speak for fear that the floodgates would open and she would dissolve in an embarrassing flood of snotty tears. Other ranch hands and members of Amy's group began to approach to check on her, but he waved them away behind her back to keep as few people as possible from watching her, in case she suddenly lost control.

"I think so," she whimpered when she finally found her voice, taking deep breaths and fighting through the pain in her ribcage.

"Does anything feel broken?" he asked, not sure how she would know that yet as she seemed to be in some state of shock.

Amy forced herself to take an exaggerated breath to test out her ribs, wincing as the skin stretched slowly along her ribs. She let out the tiniest cry as she inflated her lungs to capacity, but shook her head when Carey looked alarmed. "I think I'm just really scraped up. I don't think anything's broken," she answered, her voice shaking now that the possibility of what could have happened finally dawned on her.

Carey held her close to him, watching her carefully. He urged his horse forward in a slow walk heading toward the RV so Amy could be checked out, but didn't want her to be frightened by the sideways position in which she rode. She let her headrest against Carey's shoulder and closed her eyes, too nervous to watch after being dragged. Her heartbeat slowly began to come back down to something close to normal, no thanks to being held in Carey's arms.

When they approached the RV, Carey called out to his horse to stop before swinging one leg over and jumping to the ground, pulling Amy with him in his arms as though he did this every day. She embarrassed herself by grabbing frantically at the fabric of Carey's sleeves as they started down, and was slightly more embarrassed when she realized that Carey wasn't going to put her on the ground. Instead, he smiled at her reassuringly and knocked on the door of the trailer with the toe of his boot, then waited patiently for someone to open it, holding her the entire time.

"You don't have to do that, I think I can walk," she said quietly, more upset from the fear than from her injuries. As much as she had thought about Carey holding her so close to him, this wasn't how she'd wanted it to happen.

"And miss a chance to hold a pretty girl? Never," Carey answered kindly, hoping his humor would calm her nerves or distract her from what had just happened. "The last time I had to haul someone off who'd been dragged half to death, it was a big, smelly, hairy guy. He was no picnic, let me tell you. I'm not missing this for the world! In fact, I might just hold you the whole time the medic checks you over!" His perfect smile was disarming, letting Amy forget for a second—maybe just a millisecond—about the pain and the fear.

Bernard opened the door to the trailer and looked amused at the sight of his son holding a beautiful woman in his arms, almost as though he was about to cross the threshold with her, but his expression quickly changed when he saw the look of hurt and distress on her face. "What happened? Are you all right?"

Amy nodded tearfully, but Carey was quick to explain. He walked through the narrow trailer door, telling his father to radio for their medic to join them. He carefully sat Amy on the bench seat inside, then stepped into the bedroom at the rear of the camper and came back out with one of his father's clean undershirts. Using the knife from his belt, Carey cut a series of slits in the shirt while Bernard stared on, wondering what was happening to his laundry.

When Carey had finished, he held it out and came over to Amy. "Here, we'll tie this around behind your neck, and tie this part here down around your waist." He got to work on the makeshift straps he'd made, lifting her hair and tying it carefully so as not to pull any of her curls. When he finished, he stepped back and surveyed what looked a lot like an oversized bib, leaving Amy and Bernard speechless.

"Son, what'd you just do to my shirt?" Bernard demanded, making Amy laugh a little bit until she caught herself, holding her sides painfully.

"Um, well, it's because she's gonna have to take her shirt off, Dad," Carey answered pointedly, not wanting to embarrass Amy. "I'm sure she doesn't want to sit here half-dressed with Jerry coming in here to check on her."

As she recognized what Carey had done, Amy relaxed a little and thanked him. "That was really thoughtful, thanks. And thank you for donating your shirt, sir, even if you didn't know you were going to!"

Bernard laughed at her remark, patting Carey on the back. "It's all right, ma'am," Bernard replied, tipping his hat to her briefly. "I'm happy to give up a shirt if it keeps you comfortable. Now, let me go see what's keeping Jerry from checking on you."

After the door closed behind Bernard, Amy looked up at Carey and said, "No, really. I meant it. Thanks, that was incredibly thoughtful of you. Most guys wouldn't have thought of that."

"Well, it's not like your shirt was going to survive anyway, not with all the tears in the back, but I know Jerry, and he's probably gonna start hacking it apart at the seams the second he walks through that door. We've had enough cowboys thrown from horses for me to know that he doesn't like to move anyone's shoulders without having to. It comes with the job. We have someone snap a collarbone about once a week on the ranch, and Jerry just starts slicing so he doesn't have to move 'em too much."

Just as he'd predicted, the trailer door opened and a new face walked in, a kindly looking man who looked like he'd seen plenty of sunshine and fresh air over the years. His whole face crinkled when he smiled at Amy, and Jerry crossed the small camper in two steps to kneel down in front of her.

"So, you thought you'd try trick riding for the circus, from what I hear. I think you'd be safer doing the trapeze act, personally!" he joked with her, lifting the collar of her shirt to peer down the back. He started pressing on various places to gauge Amy's pain level before having her shrug her shoulders and rotate her joints.

"I'm going to guess that nothing's broken at this point, but it's entirely up to you whether or not we need to take a drive into the nearest town and have this x-rayed. I have to tell you that there could be some breaks and I can't prescribe anything, so all I have to offer you is nothing stronger than over-the-counter stuff for the hurt. It'll have to be your call," he cautioned her.

"I really don't think anything's broken," she answered. "It hurts a lot, but all of the bones feel okay." She tried to prove her point by moving her arms and neck, wincing as she pulled the muscles across her shoulder blades.

"Well, let's take a look at how torn up you got, and we'll go from there." Jerry produced a curved pair of sheers from the pocket of his cargo pants and got to work cutting away the fabric of her shirt. Carey turned around to give her some privacy, only facing her again when Jerry said he was done. He turned back just as Amy was tucking the fabric of Bernard's shirt into place. "Well, honey, did you try to slide past every cactus in the state? You look like you were going for some kind of pin cushion record!"

Amy blanched at the thought of cactus needles sticking out of her back, knowing that what goes in had to come out eventually. Carey looked over her shoulder to peek down her back, coming back up to look at her with an awful expression. "Um, Amy, I'm not sure you still have skin back there," he said, cringing.

"What?! Are you kidding me? It can't be that bad, it only hurts when I move it," she argued, alternating between the two cowboys with a shocked look.

"I'm only teasing, we both are," Carey finally revealed. "Don't get me wrong, it's bad, I mean, really, really ugly bad but then again, it's not that bad. You just have a few really red scrapes and a couple of places where the skin is broken up. Now don't go getting heroic, it's gonna really hurt down in the muscles, probably more tomorrow than today. You're gonna have to take it easy."

"Oh, goody, I've been looking for an excuse to kick back and do nothing on this trip," Amy said sarcastically, rolling her eyes at Carey to cover up the very pronounced stinging already spreading out across her back. "I didn't come all this way to lay around like a pampered pet. I'll be fine. Let's just put some ointment on it so it won't get infected, and I'll be good to go."

Carey came and knelt in front of her. "Amy, you don't have to be brave. You were dragged by a horse, for crying out loud! Take it easy for the next day or so. I tell you what, I'll take a turn driving the truck tomorrow, and you can help me navigate, okay? Just take one day away from the horse that tried to maim you? For me?"

There's a long list of things I'd do for you, Amy thought before she could help herself, pulled into the trance of his deep eyes and adding before she could stop herself, *and to you.* Amy didn't trust herself to respond, not with thoughts like that one running through her mind uncontrollably, so she simply sighed and gave Carey a look defeated resignation.

"Great!" he called as he stood and walked toward the low door. "I'm gonna see if one of the others in the group can't help me find you another shirt. How about I find you again at dinnertime? You just relax in here and let Jerry fix you up, okay?" And just like that, he was gone, leaving Amy to stare longingly at the door to the trailer and wonder how in the world she'd just ended up with a date on a cattle drive.

Carey closed the door to the RV behind him and leaned against the metal exterior, shocked at how those words had come out of nowhere. What was he doing asking one of the guests to have dinner with him? This was possibly the dumbest thing he could have done on the drive. Did he expect her to write to him once the two weeks was over? He tried to envision just waving goodbye as the group got back on the bus to the airport then going about his business at the ranch like nothing had happened, but even he knew that wasn't going to work out.

He'd felt an affection for Amy long before she nearly got herself killed but when he was riding alongside her and reaching for her hand, it wasn't just obligation that made him react. Carey was certain that this went way beyond chivalry, more into the territory of…what, exactly?

He didn't have to think about it for long. An angry shove to his shoulder jerked him from his thoughts. He whirled around to see who was asking for a fight and was shocked to see Karen standing there, her feet planted wide and her hands balled up on her hips.

"Just what the hell do you think you're doing?" she demanded, a snarl turning down the corners of her mouth. Her eyes blazed with whatever fury had her so worked up. For his part, Carey stared at her blankly.

"I don't think I know what you mean, ma'am," he began, falling back on his father's requirement that staff members be polite to the guests at all times, attempted assaults included.

32

"Don't play stupid, you're not enough smart enough for that," she shot back at him. "Is this all a big game to you, where you bring people out here and you all play Wild West with us for two weeks? Do you all go around sweeping up the damsels in distress and carting them off to the 'medicine man', or is that just something you're doing to Amy because you think she's vulnerable enough to fall for it?"

"Look," Carey started, completely dumbfounded by her accusations. "I don't know what's happened to offend you, but I 'swept up' Amy because she was about to get her forehead kicked in by a charging horse, one that was dragging her, I'd like to add." He pointed behind him to the RV. "If you'd like to step in there and take a look at her injuries for yourself, you're welcome to. But knock first, she might not want you in there."

"What is that supposed to mean?" Karen demanded, jutting out her jaw at his insinuation.

"It means exactly what I said. Amy's a big girl, and she's tougher than anyone I've had the pleasure of riding with on one of these drives. But if you think she needs rescuing from me, by all means, you can go in there and you can be the one to sweep her up and save her. I was just doing my job." He turned and stormed away before he could say something his dad would make him regret.

Chapter Five

True to his word, Carey found Amy after the rest of the afternoon's ride and lowered himself to sit beside her on the cool ground. He laughed quietly when he looked over at her and saw that she was asleep, sitting up with her dinner untouched in her lap. "Psst," he whispered close to her ear before sitting straight up, an innocent look plastered on his face. Amy jumped slightly and looked around, embarrassed at having fallen asleep during dinner.

"Tired?" he asked coolly, before taking a bite of his barbeque sandwich. Amy nodded slightly and speared a piece of potato, chewing it without looking in his direction.

"So, how's your back feeling? Are you gonna survive?" he asked lightly. She didn't respond right away, causing Carey to lean forward to see her face. "Hello? I asked how you're feeling?"

"I heard you. I also heard you earlier. I heard you when you were talking to Karen," she answered frostily. "But you don't have to be polite anymore. I know you're only doing your job.'" She took another forkful of her dinner, more for the excuse of eating to avoid having to talk to him than from actual hunger, having nearly lost her appetite altogether.

Carey was confused for a moment, but then remembered his argument with Karen. "Oh, you heard that?" he asked, his good mood sinking just a little bit. Amy silently smirked at him, then turned away and went back to eating. "That's not what I meant to say, Karen just got me really frustrated. I'm sorry, really. It came out wrong."

"Don't worry about it," Amy managed to reply before standing up. "I won't be any more trouble for you. I'll let you focus on your real work." She turned and walked away, leaving him to wonder how this had all gone horribly wrong. He considered just leaving well enough alone, certainly now that he had two different guests on this trip angry with him but when he saw the triumphant look Karen shot him, he decided to act. He jumped up and followed Amy, resisting the urge to shoot an inappropriate gesture in the witch's direction.

With her injured back, it wasn't hard to catch up to her. Carey approached her where she was standing behind one of the trucks, away from the prying eyes of the others, and touched her lightly on the arm. "Hey, Amy. Stop a second and talk to me."

"What?" she demanded sadly, angry with herself for letting Carey see how much he'd upset her when she turned and saw his face. He could tell that she seemed to be on the verge of tears. "What is it? I meant what I said, you don't have to look out for me. You have your job to do and I'll stay out of your way from now on."

"Amy, you're not in the way, and I didn't help you today because I had to. I helped you because I couldn't stand the thought of you getting hurt." Carey watched her carefully, but ignored the voice in his head that began telling him how weird he sounded, how pathetic. He shook his head and continued, no matter how ridiculous the thought of pouring his heart out to someone he'd met only days ago might be. "I don't even know you but for some reason, I've figured out that I spend a good bit of my day trying to make you smile, because your smile is the best thing I've seen in a long time."

She stared at Carey, unsure of how to respond, waiting for all of this to make sense but at the same time, hoping it would keep being so unreal. He waited for her to say something but when she stayed quiet, his heart began to drop.

"I'm sorry, I shouldn't have said that. I mean, I don't know anything about you and it's not my place to tell you these things. For all I know, you have a boyfriend back home and…"

Amy closed the distance between them and kissed Carey hungrily, not caring who was watching. *Karen could stand there and give us pointers, for all I care,* she thought as she lightly placed her hands on Carey's arms, warming inside when he returned her kiss and put his hands at her waist, drawing her closer.

"Oh, wow," she said, breaking the kiss and looking sheepish. "it's my turn to apologize…"

"No, don't apologize!" Carey insisted, his grin lighting up his face.

"I shouldn't have done that, I'm so sorry!" She looked away, embarrassed at letting his words get to her like that.

Carey stepped closer to her again, looking into her eyes and saying, "I'm really glad you did. I've wanted to kiss you since you stepped off the bus!"

Amy laughed lightly, still shocked at herself for being so bold, so out of character. "Well, I can't say the same. When I stepped off that bus, there were two of you! I wouldn't have known who to attack! But seriously, I'm sorry for throwing myself at you like that."

"Don't be sorry," Carey said quietly, taking one of her curls between his fingers and playing with its silkiness. "I'm not." She looked up at him and saw her own want reflected in his expression but this wasn't the time or the place, especially not now that she could hear voices approaching the vehicle. Amy decided it might be best to change the subject as they stepped out from behind the truck and headed back to rejoin the group.

"I don't see how you guys do it. How do you do this much manual labor all-day and still have the energy to sit around talking and singing after dinner? It's all I can do to keep my eyes open, but I'm afraid I'm going to miss something if I close them."

36

"Well, it's not exactly like you only endured a regular day's work. Your poor little body was pretty beat up out there today. But to answer your question, we get used to it, I guess," Carey conceded. "I can only imagine how out of place I'd feel if I tried to follow you around at work for a week. You do things that I don't have to handle, you know."

"Like what?" she asked, making herself comfortable near the campfire that was beginning to take hold.

"I don't know exactly, but I'm guessing you go to the grocery store, you go out to eat, you look like you go to the gym," he said, pinching her small bicep between his fingers lightly, thrilling her as he did. "You probably go to the movies and stuff like that. Right? I don't think our cowboy lifestyle…sorry, cow human lifestyle…is any harder than your life. It's probably just different."

Amy smiled at his mention of their joke from before, then nodded thoughtfully. "Maybe you're right. I don't think anything of going to the movies at eleven o'clock at night, then getting up and going to work the next day. It's just that I don't burn anywhere near as many calories in my day-to-day life as people must do out here."

"I see you're not having your beer," Carey mentioned, gesturing to her usual tin cup of water with his hand. "You only get the one, you might want to go snag it!"

"Oh, I'm kind of a light weight. I don't drink much. And that's even when I'm not letting my horseplay piñata with me!" she laughed, trying her best to find the humor in the incident from earlier. Everyone had been very careful and cautious with her, so she knew it had to have looked pretty bad. Thinking of how funny it must have looked helped Amy focus instead on the positive, namely that she didn't crack her own head open or get stomped to death by a horse. "After the beating I took today and the headache afterward, I'll just stick to water."

"In that case, I bet there's a line of guys who would saddle your horse for you for the rest of the trip if you let them. Dad's really laid back with his staff when they're off the clock, as long as they don't get into trouble or do anything stupid. But on the drive, we're on the clock the whole time, so he has a one-drink-limit." Carey waved over one of the hands who was walking past, then turned to Amy with a questioning look. "You're sure you don't want it?"

Amy nodded. "I'm sure. I never really liked the taste anyway." Carey negotiated the bargain between Amy and the cowboy who'd been eating nearby with his back against the tire of one of the trucks, laughing when the guy took off running back to the chuck wagon to help himself to an additional drink.

"Just make sure he follows through every day," Carey warned her with another of his glorious smiles. "Because you'll be in the truck tomorrow, he might forget by the next day!"

"Do all the guys listen to you like that?" Amy asked, trying not to come off as nosy.

"What do you mean?" he asked, cocking his head in confusion.

"You know, you just tell them what to do and they go running?" she asked timidly.

"Well...no. Not really. I mean, there's some of that, where the guys kind of have to listen to me because my dad's Bernard Carson and his name's on their paychecks, but it's not just that." Carey suddenly looked uncomfortable, and it took him a minute to realize that Amy's question made him feel like a fraud, like he had stepped into his twin brother's shoes when no one was looking. People didn't listen to him, he was the younger twin...always had been, always would be. He knew it was a dynamic of his own making, certainly no one else had pushed him into the role of forgotten younger twin. For the first time, though, he began to wonder why that was, or more accurately, why he'd made that true.

"What is it then?" Amy asked, genuinely interested in what made Carey so easy-going and likeable, but still so efficient and so in charge.

"I think if you can make people want to do what you ask, then they're more inclined to. Look at us. Did I *tell* you to eat with me? If I remember it right, I didn't even ask you. I just offered to find you because you looked like you could use a little lighter conversation and a little more pleasant company. And here you are."

"Are you saying you were so charming, I wouldn't have had any other choice but to sit with you?" Amy asked coyly, even while knowing deep down that it was entirely, unavoidably true. There was something inherently charming about Carey Carson, most of it coming from the fact that he didn't seem to know how heart-stoppingly good looking he was.

"Nope. I'm saying I was hoping you'd want to eat with me, and so I just behaved that way," he said, returning her gaze. "And considering who your mealtime companions have been so far, I think I might have been the best offer you'd had yet, so here you are!" Amy nodded, remembering the constant baiting and debating going on within her group of fellow travelers over everything from religion, to politics, to women's issues. It was enough to ruin a nice, pleasant, *quiet* sunset on the prairie.

"But you said you have to make people want to do what you say. How? Do you just make people think it was their idea?" She hated that she sounded like she was prying, but this was knowledge she needed. It was exactly the kind of thing that made her sign up for this trip in the first place.

"Not at all. It comes from having the same goal in mind, from wanting the same things. We want these cattle to get to market safely, and in good health. We all want that, or these guys wouldn't be here. They just know that I wouldn't ask them to do something that wasn't in their best interests and the interests of the ranch. I don't have a power trip, I guess, and the guys know that about me."

"Well, you are a rare person these days, if you don't have any hidden agendas or power trips," she said morosely. "Far too many people these days are out to see if they can be the top dog, and they make other people prove it for them."

"That's awful, that's no way to live," Carey said quietly. "I guess there is one way that the cowboy lifestyle is different than the rest of the world. Out here, we're all just trying to make enough that we can keep doing this. Any one of these guys could find a job in a city doing hard labor, and probably make triple what they earn on the ranch. They're out here because they want to be, not because they have to be."

They finished eating the rest of their dinner in thoughtful, comfortable silence. When they finished their meals, they silently put their plates away and walked past the truck, past the blazing campfire where everyone was gathering for the evening entertainment. Without a word between them, Carey and Amy kept walking, out into the dark, away from the group, listening to the sounds of insects calling to each other around them. Carey silently reached for her hand, interlacing his warm fingers among hers. He felt her tense up at his touch before relaxing little by little.

When they reached the ridge that overlooked their camp for the night, they climbed to its small peak and sat down, looking out over the group, watching the sparks from the fire dance upward and melt in the dark. Carey pulled Amy closer to him, wrapping his arm lightly around her injured shoulders and holding her closer to him. She turned to watch his face and smiled, biting her bottom lip and silently begging him to kiss her as her eyes

40

watched his mouth hungrily. He placed one strong hand gently on her cheek, holding her carefully as he leaned down and placed his lips on hers, lightly at first but growing more eager when she parted her lips and invited him in. Their tongues met tentatively at first, their kiss growing deeper and more feverish as they gave in to the other.

Chapter Six

"I know you're in there, Carson!" Crazy Mack shouted from the yard in front of the large, two-story main house on Carson Hill Ranch. "Get your ass out here and face me!"

Another shot rang out, taking another one of the large windows with it. Mack was up to four windows so far, blasting out each of them one at a time in his rage. Anders had called the sheriff after the first shot tore through a ground floor window but even by helicopter, the police were still a good twenty minutes away.

"What does he want?" the kitchen staff's lead assistant asked from where they were crouched in the oversized, windowless kitchen where Anders had herded them all to safety. Even for someone so young, he'd been smart enough to order them all into the large room and down on the floor when the first window was taken out. They were all too happy to comply, especially with the shouting coming from outside the house.

"I can't be sure, in his state of mind," Anders began. "but I'm willing to bet that it has something to do with his two hookers going missing and showing up here a couple of weeks ago."

"Please don't call them that," one of the housekeepers said sternly, looking at Anders reproachfully.

"That's what they are," he argued defensively. "They said so themselves."

"It doesn't matter, we still don't call them that. First of all, there are more polite terms than 'hooker'," she reprimanded, making a screwed up face as she spit out that word. "but it's just not necessary to refer to them that way. You can't know what those poor girls have been through, practically being held prisoner by that man and being forced to..."

"I'm sorry, you're right," Anders muttered. "That wasn't polite. His two girls, then. I mean, the girls, not his girls." Everyone nodded thoughtfully, remembering how sickly and abused the two girls had looked when they showed up on the porch, refusing to come inside as they waited as though they knew they weren't clean enough or good enough.

The girls in question, Emma and Dee, had snuck out of Mack's bar and walked all the way from Hale, over an hour away by car, just to warn Casey and Miranda that her violent ex-boyfriend had tracked her down in Texas. When Mack discovered his two sources of additional income missing, word got back to him that the pair were holed up somewhere on the Carson's property. At that moment, they were hidden safely in a cabin to the east, struggling against the addiction that had kept them chained to him, with the help of a retired counselor Bernard had sent to stay with them.

The sound of a loud bang followed by tinkling glass let them know that Crazy Mack was living up to his moniker by shooting out another of the first floor windows.

"Where is Sheriff Matthews?" One of the kitchen workers cried softly, putting her hands over her ears and closing her eyes. "Shouldn't he be here by now?" The older housekeeper put her arm around the younger woman, shushing her soothingly and rocking slowly.

"Don't worry, he'll get here soon and handle this," Anders promised her. He calculated the situation, then said, "Crazy Mack hasn't come inside because he doesn't know how many of us are still here. That's why he's standing in the yard, playing tough guy with that gun. He knows almost everyone is on the drive, including Dad. That's why he hasn't tried to come in. If he were to come inside, he knows that any of the six of us boys could still be here."

"Then what's he doing? What's the point of this?" The housekeeper demanded pleadingly as another window took a hit. She threw her hands over her ears and closed her eyes tightly.

"He's just showing his muscle, trying to frighten the...girls...because he thinks they're here. Plus, he knows we'll let Dad know about this, and maybe get him to head home. Everyone in town knows the drive was started, and everyone also knows Dad never misses it. Mack is just putting on a show and making himself feel better. He has to feel like he did something about this."

Within minutes, Anders held a finger to his lips to caution the seven of them not to make a sound. He heard a sound in the distance, growing louder as it came closer. Finally, the sound of helicopter blades chopping through the air rhythmically caused him to smile.

"See? The sheriff is here so this'll be cleared up soon. Nothing to worry about." Anders strained to listen for any noise, but couldn't hear anything from within the interior, other than the sound of frightened people struggling to breathe quietly.

When a knock finally sounded on the front door, no one moved. It wasn't until the visitor announced his presence as part of the sheriff's department that they felt safe enough to come out of hiding, walking slowly together in a huddle toward the door, stepping over broken glass as they walked.

When Anders reached a hand out towards the doorknob, the elderly head housekeeper moved to stop him. "You might be the only Carson and the only male around, but I'm still the oldest and I'm responsible for you. I could never forgive myself if I let your mother down by letting something happen to you. Now, step back, young man." She pushed Anders lightly, nodding when Amanda threw an arm around his young shoulders. The housekeeper silently counted to three while she watched the scared faces of the others, then opened the door a crack. She threw it open wide when she saw the deputy, barely older than Anders, pulling him inside and grabbing him in a bear hug.

"Thank God you're finally here! He's a lunatic!" She cried, pointing to the living room floor and the windows. "Look at what he's done!" The deputy nodded and began writing things in a small black notebook, shaking his head when all of the staff began talking at once.

"Where's the sheriff?" Amanda asked, looking over the deputy's shoulder like that would explain his absence. "Crazy Mack comes out here shooting at us, and Matthews sends a kid to save us?"

The deputy wasn't even old enough to be offended by the remark. He began trying to explain that the sheriff was going to take the helicopter and try to locate the shooter, and that the deputy would spend the night out there with them.

"I'll be outside, walking patrol around the place. Don't worry, we're going to take good care of you," he assured them, but the expressions on their faces said they clearly didn't feel all that protected. They looked at each other, the housekeeper grumbling about how they'd need to stay in the kitchen because they only had Deputy Diaper Pants to protect them. That remark finally hit home, causing the young officer to blush a beet red. They turned away and went back in the kitchen to spend a sleepless night on its cold floor.

Chapter Seven

Carey laid on his back in his sleeping bag, his hands behind his head as he looked up at the stars. These were the same stars he saw every night on the wide, unbroken expanse of sky back home, but there was always something magical about seeing them on the drive. It was times like this when he understood his dad's love of the old style cattle drive, the way he felt connected to all the generations of Carsons who'd worked this ranch before him. It was easy to forget what it was like for those cowboys, the days of hauling water and cooking all of the meals over a fire in the yard having long since been replaced by modern conveniences.

He usually had no trouble sleeping on a drive, even on the hard surface beneath the grassy area, because the days of backbreaking work and spending hours in the saddle tended to make anyone pass out before hitting the ground. But something was different this time, and it wasn't just missing his brother, Casey. He knew it had to be that girl, and he knew that was dangerous ground. She'd be returning to her real life in a couple days, so what was the point in getting closer to her?

But the way she'd felt when he kissed her, shy but wanting, wasn't a feeling Carey could easily forget. He'd been too surprised and too respectful to move past anything other than that kiss but the scent of her, the feel of her smooth skin beneath his hands, weren't sensations he was likely to forget any time soon.

You just have romance on the brain since Dad started his pet project, Carey told himself. *You're here to work, not to hook up with a girl who came out here to find herself for a week.*

As if even fate was working against him, Carey was startled by a rustling noise nearby. He turned his head to find the source of the sound, but couldn't make out anything in the dark of the moonless night. Finally, the rustling grew closer and a warm hand reached out to touch his bare shoulder.

"Shhh, it's only me," Amy whispered, leaning close enough to him that he caught the wonderful scent of her as her loose hair brushed his skin. He reached up and pulled her closer, cradling her to him as his mouth found hers.

"What are you doing here?" he asked finally, his breath hot against her ear as he whispered to her.

"I'm doing what you said," she answered in a confident whisper. "I'm letting you know what I want, and hoping you want the same thing." Carey could practically hear the smile in her voice as she spoke. He quietly unzipped his sleeping bag and let her slip in with him, pulling the thick fabric around their shoulders as he cradled her close to his chest.

"I know what I want," Carey replied in a husky voice, thick with want and emotion, but spoken so softly as to not call attention to them. "But not here, not some quick romp in the middle of all these sleeping people. You're worth waiting for, even if patience is painful!"

"Painful?" she asked coyly, placing a long kiss on the underside of his jaw and smiling triumphantly to herself when he shuddered.

"Deadly, even. I might actually die, and it would be on your conscience," he whispered.

Carey pressed her to him, entranced by the way their bodies fit together perfectly. Even in the close quarters of his sleeping bag, he felt like he couldn't bring her close enough, wanting to pull her even closer somehow.

He kissed her for what seemed like hours, Amy running her hands over the muscled ridges in his arms and his chest, exploring him in the darkness. She wondered at the heated softness of the skin beneath his t-shirt, tracing the pronounced muscles in his back with her delicate fingertips. She finally worked her way up to place her hands on his neck, joining them behind him and twirling locks of his luxurious hair between her fingers.

The sound of a rock being kicked across a patch of dirt nearby made Amy and Carey freeze, him putting one fingertip to her mouth as he listened. Carey looked up to see the beam of a flashlight shining across the ground in wide arcs, sweeping over the forms of sleeping cowboys. He pulled the edge of his sleeping bag up over Amy's head, suppressing a giggle when she used the cover of darkness to place the ends of her fingers on his ribs, knowing he couldn't say or do anything to stop her.

"Carey?" Bernard called out quietly, looking over the sleeping ranchers for him.

"Yeah, Dad?" he called out in a voice heavy with false sleepiness. Bernard turned toward Carey's voice and approached him, stepping around different bodies in his path.

"I need you to get up and come meet me in the RV."

"What's wrong?" Carey asked, forgetting his romantic antics for a minute and sounding concerned. He kept the cover over Amy, but was troubled by the sound of his dad's worried voice.

"We'll talk when you make it inside. Hurry." Bernard switched off his flashlight, freeing Amy to come up for air. He turned and went back to his truck without waiting for Carey to get dressed and follow him.

"Is everything okay?" Amy whispered against Carey's neck, letting her lips pause there as he answered. Carey hugged her close, but shook his head.

"I'm not sure. He doesn't usually do that, and he sure sounds worried. I'm sorry, but I'd better go see what he needs." Carey unzipped his sleeping bag and helped Amy out, then followed her, shaking out his boots and sliding them over his sock feet. He kissed her passionately one last time, then took off at a light run to the well-lit truck.

"What's up, Dad?" Carey asked, pulling the door to the RV shut after watching to make sure Amy made it safely back to where she was supposed to be sleeping.

"There's been trouble back at the house," the older man said darkly, anger on his face. He held the satellite phone tightly in his hand, listening for his younger son to come back on.

"What kind of trouble?" Carey demanded, immediately concerned. Only a handful of the staff had stayed behind, mostly women and older ones at that, people who had no interest in riding all day and sleeping on the ground every night. Plus, Anders had stayed behind, as usual, to help oversee the business end of things, which was good considering his health problems and his allergies, very real concerns that had plagued him since his difficult birth.

"They think Crazy Mack came out there. He started shooting up the house, screaming like…well…a crazy man."

"Are you kidding? He shot at them? Is everyone okay?" he stormed, beginning to pace back and forth within the small space of the RV. "Who's out there now?"

Anders' tiny voice came through the speaker. "Sheriff Matthews came out, but Mack took off when he saw the helicopter. No one's really hurt, but Meg had to go into town to the doctor. She cut her hand trying to clean up some of the glass but she'll back in the morning, just had to get a few stitches. It looks like he shot out about eight or nine of the windows, and I haven't been outside to see if he did any damage to the other buildings or if he shot any of the animals that are still around here."

"Don't go out there, Anders!" Bernard yelled. "Stay in the house, and keep everyone else inside, at least until Matthews has a chance to find this lunatic!"

"Okay, Dad," Anders replied. He could be heard through the connection talking to some people in the background before coming back to address them. "The sheriff is going to leave someone here tonight, but the deputy will have to go back to town in the morning."

"Don't worry, son, we'll have someone home by late tomorrow night, maybe the next morning. You guys try to get some sleep and have everyone sleep in the main house. Don't let any of the staff go back out to their quarters until this is all cleared up."

Bernard signed off and switched off the phone before turning to Carey. "Son, I need you to head back home."

"Really? Why?" he asked, confused for a moment before realizing for the hundredth time that he was the oldest now. "Oh, right. Sure, I'll get my stuff and leave right now."

"No, you need some sleep before you can head out. Take my bed in there. I want you to be well rested because you'll most likely have to drive straight through. I'll sleep out here on the bench seat." Carey nodded, then went into the bedroom at the far end of the RV and did as he was told, so worried about his younger brother and the staff back home that he had to force himself to close his eyes and get some much needed rest.

He was awakened by someone shaking him softly, calling his name over and over. Carey opened his eyes to see his father's face above him, a pitch-black sky still visible outside the windows. He rubbed the sleep from his eyes and pulled his t-shirt on over his head, getting out of bed and finishing getting dressed before stepping over to the coffee maker on the small kitchen counter.

"Take the truck," Bernard said. "and call me along the way. I'll let you know what Anders has reported. Do you need to take Dwayne with you?"

"Well, it'd be nice to have another driver and to have some more muscle on the ranch when we get there, but I'm afraid you can't spare him. No, you'll need him for the rest of the drive, especially without Casey or me. I'll just have to go on through."

"Promise me you'll pull over and nap if you get tired, Carey," his dad pleaded sternly. "Nothing will be resolved if you don't make it there in one piece, and I sure don't want anything to happen to you out on the road."

"I'll be fine. I promise I'll be careful," he assured him, but he was too keyed up with worry to guarantee he'd be that cautious. Knowing that Mack hadn't been found meant he was more than likely still hiding out somewhere on the ranch, and there was no telling what he'd be stupid enough to try once darkness fell again.

Carey stepped out of the RV and immediately spotted Amy, rolling up her sleeping bag by the remains of last night's campfire. He felt a pull in his gut at the thought of not seeing her for the rest of the ride, and of just leaving things hanging with this stranger he'd only just met. He walked up to her, completely undone by her bright smile, only to feel crushed when her face fell, sensing that something was wrong by the look on his face.

"I have to leave," Carey began. "I'm sorry. I hope you have a great rest of your trip, and a safe trip back home." He started to turn to leave, but she put a hand on his arm to stop him.

"Carey, is something wrong? Why are you leaving?" she asked calmly, not so much for her own benefit but because she could see something was really troubling him.

"Um, it's just some problems back at the ranch. My younger brother is there and there's been a...an incident. Kind of an emergency. I'm driving back now, and hope I get there without having to stop anywhere. Again, I really am sorry we didn't get to spend more time together. I would really have liked to get to know you better." He turned and walked toward the truck, turning back once sadly to see Amy still standing, watching him go.

"Carey, wait!" She finally called, running behind him. "I'll go with you."

"What? You can't just cancel your trip. No, don't be silly. Stay here and enjoy the rest of the drive."

"Have you seen me on a horse? What part of that looks like I'm enjoying it? And I know for sure the horse isn't loving it. We'll switch off driving and you can get there faster if you don't have to worry about being rested."

"Amy, really, I appreciate it, but..."

"...but you don't want me to go," she finished for him, dropping her voice. "Oh. I see. I'm sorry, I didn't mean to intrude. Go ahead." She stepped back and looked around awkwardly, embarrassed at Carey's rejection.

"No, that's not it!" He promised, coming back to her and putting a hand on her shoulder. "I just can't ask you to get involved in this. There's a...situation...back home. Someone's already attacked the house, and I can't put you in danger."

"I don't mind that, as long as you're sure that's all it is. If you don't want me to go, I'll butt out, but if you want to make it there before dark, I can help. I want to help." Amy looked at him confidently, none of her former wallflower showing through anymore. Carey watched her face for only a moment, then nodded.

"Come on, throw your stuff in the truck. We have to leave in about five minutes. I'll wait over here."

Amy nodded, all business now that she was helping out, and ran to retrieve her things. Not even a nasty remark from Karen about how Amy was chasing after him and throwing herself at an "oppressor" could dampen her mood. She was glad to be getting off this rather difficult and disappointing cattle drive, no matter how desperate the circumstances that caused it, and the added benefit was that she would be spending this time with Carey.

By the time she returned, Carey was stepping into the driver's seat of a rather large truck. She shook her head, jerking her thumb at the passenger seat. "Uh-uh, mister, you only had a couple of hours' sleep. Let me start out first, and you can sleep in the back seat."

"Amy, I just realized something. You have to have a CDL license to drive this kind of truck. I don't think you're going to want to manage it," Carey said, wincing at having already promised her she could help out.

"For your information," she began sarcastically, jutting out her hip and slapping her hand on her waist. "I happen to have a CDL license. And I've driven vehicles far bigger than this little thing. So slide yourself over there, get that sweatshirt under your head, and let me hear some snoring, cowboy!"

Amy flashed Carey a knowing look and climbed in the driver's seat, leaving him dumbfounded as he resorted to getting in the back. He started to tell her how to use the GPS, but realized she probably knew how to work something as simple as that. After peeking over the top of the seat to make sure she was headed in the right direction on the highway, he laid back and closed his eyes for just a moment but sat ramrod straight when he felt how fast they were going.

"Amy! Slow down! You're doing almost a hundred miles an hour!" Carey called out nervously.

"It's okay, Carey, I have this. This is nothing for me," she answered calmly, checking her mirror before crossing the centerline to pass someone in her lane. She moved back over and kept going, the wind rushing past the windows making a dull roar that followed them.

Within only minutes, a police car pulled out behind them, lights and sirens blaring. Carey began to sweat, aware for the first time that he couldn't actually remember Amy's last name from her paperwork. Amy pulled over and reached into her purse for her wallet, appearing as calm as if she were simply looking for a pack of gum.

"Hi, Officer," Amy began, flipping through her wallet for her identification.

"I hope you have a really good explanation for the way you're driving, missy," the older deputy said with a drawling sneer.

"I do, sir. My name is Officer Amy McDade, Detroit PD," she said, handing over her badge. "This passenger is Carey Carson, of the Carson Hill Ranch outside Hale, Texas. There's been a shooting and attempted home invasion at his family's ranch, and the only family member on the premises is a minor child, aged sixteen, in the care of some of the family's ranch staff. The local sheriff's department has already been on the scene but the shooter wasn't apprehended. We have reason to believe he may be hiding on the property, and because the motive for the shooting was revenge, we need to get there in a hurry."

The officer took her badge and looked it over, holding it up to the light, alternating between looking at the badge and the driver's license, and looking at Amy's sweet face. Carey sat still, his mouth open in shock.

"Lemme call this in," the officer said, moseying back to his squad car. He returned only a few minutes later, handing the badge and ID through the open driver's window. "If you'll put on your hazard lights, ma'am, I'm to escort you to the county line, where the Cangor County sheriff's deputy will take over. We'll get you to Hale in no time."

The officer returned to his car and put on his lights and siren, then flew around their parked truck, waving her on. Amy pulled back out onto the highway and followed the officer as closely as she dared.

"You're supposed to be asleep, you know," Amy said playfully after spotting Carey in the rear view mirror.

"Are you kidding? How am I supposed to sleep at a time like this? Why didn't you tell me you're a cop?" Carey asked in succession, surprised at every new piece of information he slowly learned about this woman.

"Was that information you needed?" She asked, a smile still playing at the corners of her mouth. "It just never came up, what with all the kissing and the touching and the tongues in each other's mouths."

"But tell me this…if you're some bad-assed big city cop—pardon my expression, sorry—why are you out here trying to build your confidence up? It's the cows that should have been afraid of you, not the other way around, right?"

Amy was quiet for a long pause, staring straight ahead at the yellow dotted lines on the road as they disappeared under the wheels of the truck. She finally got up the nerve to explain something she had told very few people. "Because I was shot, and now I'm pretty much worthless as a patrol officer. I work at a desk all day, despite being one of the most highly trained and highly decorated women on the police force. I needed to get out of my comfort level and do something risky, something I've never tried before.

"I tried skydiving but I didn't really have to do anything there except fall. I've tried scuba diving but unless I wanted to actually get in a giant tank filled with sharks, it was just a swim during a gorgeous vacation. I have to try something new that will make me feel like I can do anything, just so I can get back to doing the thing I used to love. Now, go to sleep, you're taking over in six hours."

Carey did as he was told but instead of closing his eyes, he stared at the back of Amy's neck as she drove, watching the way one sweaty curl had escaped from her ponytail and was plastered to the back of her neck. He wanted to reach out his hand and free that sprig of hair, then caress the skin that ran down into her shirt collar, disappearing down her back, following that hand with his mouth…

When he awoke hours later, Carey sat up with a start and looked around at the landscape. He stretched as best he could in the cramped back seat, then climbed over into the front and buckled himself into the passenger seat.

"Hi, Sleeping Beauty," Amy said with a smirk. "I never pegged you for a snorer."

"I don't snore," he retorted, "that's my alarm system. I'm simply letting everyone know not to bother me because I'm asleep. Where are we?"

"Well, I don't know a lot about this part of the country, so you'll have to check the GPS. I do know we're on our eleventh cop, so we're at least eleven jurisdictions from where we started out. Are you ready to drive for a little bit? We can swap when you're good and awake."

"Yeah, that'll be fine. Amy…thanks." He ducked his head, suddenly embarrassed.

"You're welcome," she answered with a sweet smile. "But for what?"

"For all of this. For offering to come along, for arranging our very own police escort…you're pretty amazing, you know that, right?" Carey looked over at her with a sincere look of appreciation, one arm resting on the seat back between them and playing with a strand of hair that had fallen out from under her hat at some point during the long drive.

"I don't know about amazing. How about competent? I'm competent, I can admit to that." She smirked at him without taking her eyes off the road.

"You're not giving yourself enough credit. We'll meet in the middle with incredible, "how's that?"

"That's not a compromise!" Amy said, laughing and swatting at Carey playfully. "There's no way that incredible is the halfway point. How about 'semi-mediocre'?"

"Nope, not good enough. I'm the one giving compliments around here, so I get to have the majority vote. And I say that 'celestial status' is up on the list, along with extremely kind, very quick thinking, and stunningly beautiful."

Amy didn't speak for a moment, watching the squad car in front of her intently. Finally, she spoke, but when she did, her voice was somewhat hoarse with emotion. "Thank you, Carey, for what you said."

"You don't have to thank me, it's the truth," he replied, rubbing the back of her neck with his hand. She rolled her shoulders under his soft touch and stretched her back forward. "Are you ready for me to drive?"

"Sure," she answered, engaging the cruise control and checking the mirrors. "Slide over here." Carey looked around nervously before taking off his seat belt and sliding across the bench seat toward her. "Hold the wheel, don't touch the brake but be ready to hit it if necessary." Carey held the steering wheel as Amy unbuckled her seatbelt, then used her feet to push against the seat and slide over into the back seat directly behind her. Carey slid into place and buckled up as Amy came back over the seat on the passenger side.

"That was a pretty slick move, Officer McDade. How'd you learn to do that? Is that a cop thing?" he asked, watching her get comfortable in what had been his seat only seconds before. She shrugged her shoulders before responding.

"I've had years of defensive driving training, but that particular move is just something that my brothers and I would do if we needed to take turns. We used to deliver products all over Michigan for my dad's company, and the route could get pretty tedious if you didn't have someone to trade off with." Amy reached her arm across the seat back that had held Carey's arm before. "Weren't you sitting somewhere like this, maybe?" she asked, toying with Carey's shaggy hair, running her nails gently up his scalp and causing him to lean into her hand.

"Something like that, maybe a little bit to my left. Yup, that's what I was doing," he answered, smiling at Amy without taking his eyes off the road.

"I don't know," she argued in a smooth voice. "I think maybe you were over here, right?" Amy demonstrated by moving closer to Carey, close enough to breathe heavily on his neck before placing her lips against his shivering skin. She moved up his neck to his ear, where she bit down gently on his earlobe before soothing it by sucking it into her mouth.

"I would love to tell you not to stop," Carey began, forgetting to finish his sentence as Amy bit down gently on the muscle that ran on the outside of his neck.

"Yes? You were saying something about me stopping?" she asked innocently enough.

"Um…no, no I wasn't."

"I'm pretty sure I heard you say the word 'stop'," she said with a laugh, a seductive sound that was almost as maddening as what she was physically doing to him.

"No, that must have been some other guy. Don't stop," Carey half-begged, gripping the steering wheel so hard with both hands that his knuckles turned white.

"Actually, I think I should sit over here and behave myself," Amy suggested, sitting up and sliding back to her side of the truck. "That policeman won't be too happy with you if he looks in his rear-view mirror."

"Me? I'm just sitting here, innocently driving a truck over a hundred miles an hour. You're the incredible vixen sucking on my neck."

"It's just so suckable," she shot back with a satisfied giggle as Carey struggled to keep his composure. "But truthfully, I shouldn't distract you when you're driving. It's not very responsible of either of us. Tell me about your ranch instead."

Amy kept Carey talking, partly to keep him awake and focused, but also because she was genuinely interested in life out west. She was shocked by some of the things ranching required, like homeschooling because the town was so far away, and Carey learning to shoot a gun at only seven years old. Other things made the farm seem so natural and normal, mostly the way he talked about his life like it was so commonplace.

"But what about you, Miss Big City Policewoman? You must have more than enough excitement to last you a lifetime." Carey kept his eyes focused on the squad car in front of him so he wouldn't have to look at the speedometer.

"Well, it used to be exciting. I'm kind of gun-shy now, I'm afraid. I am spooked too easily, I'm too cautious." Amy looked straight ahead, not focusing on anything in particular as her mind wandered to her job.

"How can being cautious be a bad thing when you're an armed policeman? Doesn't being alert and careful mean everything in that line of work?"

"Yes, but you can be too careful. I reached the point that I'd call for back up just to check out a simple domestic dispute or a shoplifting. It wasn't fair to my partner to be saddled with someone who couldn't evaluate the situation and determine the level of risk. So I took myself off the street and agreed to work the desk. But I've been at that job so long, now I'm afraid I'll never go back."

It was Carey's turn to ask the questions without being rude or prying. "And the cattle drive was supposed to cure you? That's a pretty tall order for some very large, not very bright animals, don't you think?" he asked.

"Not cure me, exactly, but make me realize that I am capable and strong, that I can make decisions on my feet and assess a situation in the right frame of mind."

"Wow. Now I feel bad for letting you talk me into coming to the ranch. Maybe you needed a few more days on the drive, and you could have gotten your head back where you want it."

"I don't think that would have done it," Amy admitted sadly. "The drive was kind of a last-ditch effort to figure out my next career move. If I didn't come back to work as a whole new person, I was going to put in for a transfer or start looking for another jurisdiction. Maybe that gun shot came at just the right time in my career...I'd already proven I'm tough and I'm capable, and that may have been what I needed on my résumé to get my foot in the door somewhere else, somewhere a little less...intense." Amy looked out the window and was quiet after that, a fact that Carey couldn't help but think had less to do with talking herself out and more to do with a heavy weight pressing down on her.

"Then you know I do need you on this trip, and I don't just mean for the driving. We're walking straight into the lion's mouth on this, what with Mack possibly hiding out somewhere on the ranch."

Amy went into full-on investigative mode without even realizing it. "Do you have any idea of why he'd be out there for revenge? What prompted him to start shooting up the place?"

Carey told Amy the long story of two of Mack's girls showing up on the ranch and seeking shelter. He even told her where the girls were at that moment, how far from the property they would be, who knew about their whereabouts, and such. Amy nodded as Carey talked, taking it all in.

"So your dad just gave them a cabin to stay in, and hired a counselor to look after them? He's either a saint or he has an interest in getting those girls away from Mack for some reason."

Carey bristled slightly, not sure what Amy meant but had the impression that she insinuated Bernard's involvement went beyond just helping out. "What are you saying about my dad, exactly?"

"I'm saying he's putting himself and his entire family and staff at risk by taking in two females with a history of drug addiction and criminal activity. And judging by the very circumstances we're speeding into, I'd say he either didn't know the full extent of his actions, or he had a reason to act in the first place."

Carey chewed that over thoughtfully, fighting the urge to let his anger boil up at the callous way Amy assessed people she'd never even met. "You've met my father, even if it was only for a few minutes at a time. There's not an evil, hard-hearted bone in his body. Two pitiful, frightened girls—still practically kids—showed up on his doorstep after having walked almost forty miles to warn his family of a threat, and he gave them food, shelter, and assistance. I don't want to meet the man who wouldn't do exactly the same thing."

Amy was quiet, staring out the window as she thought about Carey's reaction. True, she didn't know his father at all, and true, she might have let her work get in the way of seeing someone's basic human kindness. Had her years as a cop and her struggles to fit in with some of the more aggressive, streetwise officers really made her so jaded that she couldn't believe an elderly man might do something kind for two strung out, teenage runaways?

"Hey, I'm sorry. I didn't mean to sound judgmental, and I certainly didn't mean to imply that your dad was anything but an honest, caring person. It's easy to see where you get your sensitive side." Amy smiled genuinely and waited, not pressing the issue after upsetting Carey so much. He paused before answering her, but finally spoke.

"I'm sorry, too. I guess I just got really defensive. And I can admit that the whole thing might look suspicious to an outsider, but you'd just have to know my dad the way I do. He would rather die than turn someone away, especially someone in so much need." Carey looked a little relieved to hear her explanation, but was still on edge at where the conversation had gone. *That's why Casey's so good in these situations*, he thought, wishing, once again, that his older brother was there to handle all of these things. *He's better at being...diplomatic...and boy, could I use someone who can take charge right now.*

Chapter Eight

"Anders? Anders, please answer…" Bernard called again into the small handheld unit. It had been three hours since he'd last heard anything from Carson Hill Ranch. Both of his foremen paced around the small living space of the RV, their faces creased with worry as they tried to avoid bumping into each other as they paced. Terry bit nervously at a hangnail as he walked, not looking at his boss, too upset by the desperate look on the old man's face as he tried yet again to talk to his son.

"It could be anything," Dwayne said in his most reassuring voice. "Maybe the battery ran down on it. Maybe there's a storm back home and the satellite's not picking up, just like with the TV when it rains too hard. You can't know why he's not answering."

Bernard ignored their attempts to make him feel better, certain that something was horribly wrong. Joseph sat next to his father without speaking, his leg bouncing up and down so hard underneath the table that the pens and papers moved around its surface. No one seemed to notice or care.

"All we can do is wait 'til Carey gets back and reports in with some news," Dwayne continued kindly. "There's no sense letting it eat at you until we know something for sure."

"How's this going to affect the cattle drive, Boss?" Terry asked, trying hard not to seem uncaring, but needing some clarification about their jobs. They had 30,000 head to move and were now short Carey, as well as Casey. Regardless of what the vacationers wanted to do, there was the very real consideration of selling the herd and if they didn't arrive on time, there'd be some angry brokers to deal with down the road.

"I just don't know, Terry. I can't even think about that right now. What if something happened?" Bernard asked without really speaking to anyone, staring at the useless phone in his hand as if it had betrayed him.

"Boss," Dwayne said firmly, coming over to sit down across from the old man. "I know everything's gonna be fine. There's some explanation for this, and we're all gonna laugh about how this gave you another patch of gray hair. I know he's gonna be okay. They all will." Bernard smiled and reached a weathered hand across the table to grasp Dwayne's in his own.

"Thank you. I just wish I had half the confidence you have. All I have is a really bad feeling in the pit of my stomach. I never should have left Anders behind. And all those staff members, I basically left an unarmed crew of women and a sickly teenage boy to fend for themselves against a dangerous, desperate man."

"Hey, now," Dwayne argued, trying to lift Bernard's spirits. "my wife is a member of that 'crew of women' and I feel for any man, dangerous or not, who tries to get in that house with her around. She's gonna look after Anders, and the rest of 'em, too. You've known Amanda as long as I have, and I'll tell you what, I almost feel sorry for Crazy Mack!" The foreman smiled at Bernard, putting aside his own fears for his wife for a moment, long enough to reassure the old rancher.

"Yes, I know what a spitfire Amanda is. Thank you, Dwayne. And I'm sorry I put your family in this situation." Bernard looked even more morose than before, realizing how selfish he must have sounded for worrying only about his own son when it was his staff members' families who were in harm's way as well.

"You didn't do anything, sir, it's all that nutcase's doing. We're all gonna be just fine, and this will be just one more story for us to tell around the fire at the end of the day. 'Course, by the time it gets out, we'll have a great yarn to share, with all kinds of antics and super-sized whoppers to go with it. You'll see, it's gonna be fine."

Dwayne stood and patted Bernard firmly on the shoulder before making his way out of the RV. He climbed down the metal steps and managed to get a hundred yards or so away from the truck and the rest of the group before breaking down, squatting down in the dirt and putting one hand over his moist eyes.

"Dear Lord, please let them be okay...please let Amanda be okay..."

***

Carey and Amy arrived at the ranch—thanks to the final patrol cars that led them speeding across various county lines—just before dusk turned to night. Every light in the house must have been on, as light shone from every window that wasn't boarded up with pieces of lumber the sheriff sent out from town. The exterior flood lights were on at every corner of the house, ensuring that anyone who came up in the yard would at least be seen, if not prevented from getting closer altogether.

Carey cut the engine to the truck as close to the house as he could, telling Amy to stay in her seat and duck down until he came around to her side. She might be the officer here but he was the cowboy, and no cowboy would let a woman run out into what could easily be sniper fire from a deranged, vengeful troublemaker.

He opened her door and helped her down, then threw an arm around her head and shoulders and led her hunched over into the main house. The door was locked, and he fumbled with the key from his belt for a moment, his nerves almost getting the best of him as he turned it.

"Anders! Anders! Where are you? ANDERS!" Carey shouted, running from room to room, calling out for his brother. He ran up the stairs and looked in all the bedrooms, yelling for anyone who might still be there. Amy stood by helplessly, looking around her from where she still stood in the doorway. A flash of shadow passing under the kitchen door caught her attention.

"Carey! Down here!" She called out, waiting with one hand on the stair railing for him to come downstairs. Together, they approached the kitchen door, Carey sucking in a deep breath when Amy pulled a handgun from a holster under her pants leg. His eyes grew wide as he pointed wordlessly to the gun, but Amy only shrugged.

"There's no need to be quiet, anyone in the kitchen already knows we're in here," she said. Amy used the butt of the handgun to knock on the kitchen door, then announced them. The door opened a crack, then was flung open as Anders rushed out and into his brother's arms. Carey heard the click of the safety re-engaging as Amy pulled the gun back to shoulder height before slipping it back in its holster, hopefully before Anders had a chance to see it.

"Carey, I'm so glad you're here," Anders began, his voice cracking a little bit from the emotion. He was obviously rattled, and grateful to have someone older and more experienced to take over being in charge. "I didn't know what else to do, so we've all just stayed holed up in the kitchen since last night. I figured it's where the food and water is, and there's a hallway to a bathroom. We even slept in there so we could duck between the refrigerators if Mack came back shooting."

"Anders, you're absolutely brilliant. That's exactly what you should have done. Way to take charge, little brother!" Carey said reassuringly, pulling his younger brother into his oversized hug and patting him firmly on the shoulder. The staff members who emerged from the kitchen smiled at the touching scene between brothers. Anders seemed visibly relaxed now that his big brother was home, but his face was still creased with worry lines.

"So what do we do now?" Anders asked, looking from his brother to the missing front windows.

66

"I'm not really sure. Dad just wanted me to get back down here. You guys can all take upstairs bedrooms tonight and sleep in real beds, and I'll stay awake down here. Go ahead and start rotating through the showers, too, while we're all awake." He patted Anders on the back and pushed him gently in the direction of the stairs so he could go clean up. After the kitchen staff and housekeeper had trudged wearily up the stairs, Amy approached Carey and melted into him when he pulled her tight against his chest.

"A gun? Really? In your boot?" he teased, kissing her quickly on the lips between each question. "Isn't that a little cliché, even for a big city cop?"

Amy returned his kiss before answering. "Well, we're technically never off duty, even though I'm not in my jurisdiction. But Detroit teaches you to be ready for anything, whether you're a police officer or not."

"Why don't you go upstairs and pick out a bed before everyone snags the ones with the good pillows?" Carey suggested. "I'm going to grab some blankets from the closet and fix up one of the couches down here but I'm sure I won't be able to sleep."

"Not a chance, cowboy," Amy said, shaking her head and smiling ruefully. "This is practically a stake-out. You think I'm willing to miss this? I haven't seen this much action from behind my desk in ages, I'm not about to sleep through it."

"Somehow, I didn't think you were going to," Carey added. "even before I actually suggested it! So, if you're not going upstairs to sleep…" He left his sentence hanging as he leaned down to kiss her slowly, letting his lips linger on hers before raising an eyebrow and giving Amy a smoldering look. "…what did you have planned? Hmm?"

"Well, I was thinking…" she whispered in a seductive voice, letting her eyelids fall until she peered up at Carey through her lashes. "that I would take the first watch as you slept." She kissed him again, then teasingly added in a sultry way, her lips almost touching his. "Then, I could sleep while you stayed up."

Carey laughed at her playful game, kissing her once and nodding his head. "That sounds like a good idea. Are you sure you don't want to sleep first? I don't mind staying up."

"No, you did the last part of the driving. I'm good and rested. But before you crash, are you familiar with this kind of gun? I'll pass it off to you when I go to sleep." Amy watched Carey's face for any reaction, prepared to explain why it would be necessary. Carey took her firearm and felt its weight in his hand turning it over.

"Yup, we all have to carry them out here on the ranch in case of animal attack. I was only giving you a hard time about your holster earlier. I usually wear one just like it. Not in my boot, of course, that's a new one for me, just on my belt." He kissed her one last time and hugged her tightly, then sent her off in the direction of the showers as well, pointing to his bedroom door and telling her she could get some clothes from his closet to change into while he retrieved their bags from the truck.

As the household, or what was left of it with the drovers and crew gone, settled in for some much needed sleep, Amy kept watch in a chair by the window, walking the interior of the house from time to time to check for anything out of place. She doused the lights to keep anyone outside from seeing in, and checked the locks on each door and window as she passed. Instead of feeling tense at this position of being in harm's way again, she felt oddly at home, like she was doing the job she was meant to be doing instead of the job she'd reluctantly taken after being shot in the line of duty. This was what being a cop felt like again.

She checked on every sleeping person, too, walking carefully between the beds in the upstairs room to make sure that everyone was still in place. As she moved from room to room on the second floor, the sound of breaking glass followed by a sharp thud made her spring into action. She reached the landing at the top of the stairs just as Carey woke up and began screaming.

The flames that had been launched through the window with the homemade Molotov cocktail splashed across the antique rug in the living room, sending its fiery liquid searing over Carey's flesh. She flew down the stairs and dragged him to the floor, smothering him with the blanket he'd been sleeping under.

"Get up!" Amy yelled after nothing more than smoke came from Carey's clothes. "Help me roll up this rug!" They shoved the furniture out of the way and began rolling the rug in heavy turns as the fire licked at their hands and faces. Once fully rolled, they stomped on the center of the tube-shaped rug to put out any remains of the burning gas. Finally, they dragged it into the kitchen where it wouldn't catch the hardwood floor if it was still burning, letting it rest on the cold tile floor, close enough to the sink where it could easily be doused with water.

The others ran down the stairs at the sounds of screaming, and Amy directed Anders to call Sheriff Matthews. He ran to comply as Meg retrieved several small bags of ice from the kitchen for Carey's burns. She handed them off to Carey and a look of horrified guilt crossed his face when he touched her own-bandaged hand. Meg smiled feebly, telling him it was okay.

"How bad is it?" Amy demanded, her voice shaking a little now that the adrenaline that threw her into motion was beginning to wear off. "Let me look." Instead of turning on the overheard lights and letting their attacker know where they were all congregated, she had Meg hold a flashlight over the bright pink skin that was already beginning to blister in places, bits of blackened, charred skin showing through where the chemicals had burned the hottest.

Anders returned with the phone in his hand just as Amy finished putting a loose dressing over Carey's injured arm, dabbing a bit more burn cream on the spots that ran down his cheek and his collarbone where burning drops of liquid had scorched his skin. Anders swayed slightly, looking sick when he saw the burned skin but he managed to sit down solidly before falling. The smell of burning fuel and melted carpet fibers made him start to cough and wheeze slightly.

"He needs some fresh air," Carey cautioned the others, sitting up in concern as his younger brother gasped for air. "This smoky room isn't good for him. Take him to another room, and get his inhaler!"

"We'll go upstairs and open a window just a little bit," the housekeeper offered. "We won't open it much, but I'll have him sit on the floor so he can breathe it in." The staff went with Anders to an upstairs bedroom, shutting the door behind them to keep the burning smell and smoke from following them in. Carey turned his attention back to Amy, who continued to dab ointment over his burns.

"You know, I think you just wanted to get my shirt off me," Carey joked faintly, wincing as she pressed down too hard in one spot above his collarbone. "I mean it, if that's what you wanted, all you really had to do is ask."

"I'll remember that for next time," she managed to say, trying not to tear up at the obvious pain she was causing him. "I hope I won't need anything as terrifying as a fire bomb to get you undressed in the future."

"And I hope that's not what it takes to get you to put your hands on me," he surprised himself by saying. Amy's eyes met his and she blinked back the tears, grateful that Carey could make jokes at a time like this, and even more so that he could make a pass at her, too. It meant he was probably okay.

70

"Try and stop me, cowboy," she said with a wicked grin, more to ease her own nerves than Carey's pain-ravaged ones. "But for now, you need to take these." Amy held up a small bottle of pain pills from the first aid kit, and held out her bottle of water.

"No, it'll make me fall asleep," he protested. "Someone has to stay awake with you. And then there's Anders upstairs still coughing..."

"The sheriff will be here soon," Amy argued. "Now, you get some rest. I'll wait for him."

Carey nodded grimly, knowing that Amy was making sense. "Fine, I'll take these, but not for another twenty minutes. That means I'll be falling asleep right around the time the sheriff gets here."

"You are incredibly stubborn, you know that?" Her words were meant to scold him, but Carey could tell there was a softness underneath that was all for him. He nodded, trying not to grimace in pain but failing when the raw nerves suddenly flared up again beneath the skin. "*Now* are you ready to take them?"

Carey finally nodded, giving in as a sheen of pain-induced sweat covered his injured skin, its saltiness further aggravating the burning feeling. He downed two of the pills and handed the bottle back to Amy. She felt helpless watching him cradle his arm, but knew better than to touch him and risk hurting him even more.

"Hey, why don't you tell me a story? You know, to take your mind off it?" She suggested brightly.

"What kind of story?" He asked, catching his breath.

"I don't know. What's your favorite thing about the ranch?" Amy asked, keeping him talking. "Tell me what you like best about living here."

"All the beautiful scenery," he said softly, letting his eyes lose focus for a second. "There's just so much…pretty…out here."

"Nice try, mister, but stay with me here. Those pills haven't kicked in yet, this is your own brain doing the zoning in and out. Hey! Snap up!" Amy snapped two fingers near Carey's ear, making his eyes come back into focus. She knew he was falling out, mostly from the stress of a long day and the long drive, the lack of sleep finally catching up to him. She knelt on the floor next to the couch near where his head sank against his pillow, then kissed him softly, avoiding touching any of the angry patches of burnt skin. He kissed her back longingly but during their kiss, he drifted off, his mouth going slack beneath her lips as he finally stopped feeling the pain.

Chapter Nine

Sheriff Matthews didn't arrive until the early hours of the morning and was appalled at Carey's condition. "That settles it, we're now looking at more than just vandalism and discharging a firearm. This is at least assault, if not attempted murder. That gives me more than enough reason to call in a team and help bring this guy in."

"The sooner, the better, Sheriff. Just let me know what we can do," Carey began, trying to sit up. Amy put a hand on Carey's chest to stop him as the sheriff rose up out of his chair to do the same, coming to stand in front of Carey with his hands planted on his gun belt.

"You're not going anywhere, Carey. Your father would kill me if I let any harm come to you, if he doesn't skin me alive for the way you look already. If I'd caught that son of a bitch, Mack, the first night he showed up causing trouble, you wouldn't be laying here practically turned inside out."

"Do you have any idea what brought this on, Sheriff? Why does Mack have it in for the Carsons?" Amy asked. Sheriff Matthews and Carey exchanged a silent look, but Carey's face remained unchanged. It must be all right to fill her in then.

"Well, ma'am, Mack runs a less than savory establishment over in Hale. I can't tell you how many bar fights my deputies and I have busted up in there, and there's been talk for a long time that he was running drugs through that place, but we could never pin it on him. We even started to think he was trafficking through there for a cartel south of the border. But this particular riot he's causing seems to be about two of his 'waitresses', who went missing last week. Again, I never could pin anything on him because I didn't have any complaining witnesses and because the girls both checked out as being over eighteen, but we think he was prostituting them from his bar. That's the local rumor, anyway."

"And you're sure their ID checks out?" she asked. "It'd be a whole lot easier to shut him down on suspicion if you had any reason to believe they presented fake IDs. The alcoholic beverage board would be your inroads, not the alleged prostitution. If they were using fake IDs, ones that the owner might have even made for them, then he has under-aged girls serving alcohol. That'll shut down his bar and cost him his liquor license right there." Matthews took the hint, his eyes lighting up at this new angle of investigating the bar owner.

"You know, now that you mention it, they do look awfully young. I think we'd better have a deputy do some background checks into his two employees. Where'd you say you were from, Miss…?"

"Amy McDade," she answered, sticking out her hand for a handshake. "I'm with the Detroit Police Department, I just came down here for two weeks with the 'city slickers' who join the Carson Hill cattle drive. But I ended up offering to help Carey drive back here when he heard there was some trouble."

The sheriff took her hand in his and greeted her warmly. "It's nice to have you in our part of the country, I just wish it was for sightseeing instead of holing up inside this house. If it's all right with you, Ms. McDade, how would you feel about volunteering for the Williams County Sheriff's Department while you're here? We're spread out so far over this entire region that we can't possibly have enough people, especially not with something like this going on."

"I'm happy to help, as long as I won't be in the way," Amy agreed, her eyes lighting up in a way that they hadn't in ages. The thought of getting back out in the fray was alluring, especially when a small part of her brain reminded her it was only temporary. *It's not like agreeing to go back out on my regular street patrol.*

74

This is just helping out, she told herself eagerly. *The sheriff said they were undermanned, this is practically my civic duty.*

"Not at all, just let me go make a couple of calls and check out your status with your home jurisdiction, then it'll be official. I'll feel better leaving someone out here that's authorized as part of our unit, at least during the day. Given how this coward likes to sneak around, though, we'll make sure to double up after dark. Do you have your firearm on you?" he asked, his eyes moving over her briefly as he looked for a telltale bulge of a holster.

Amy reached in the hem of her jeans for the second time since arriving at Carson Hill and retrieved her handgun, passing it to the sheriff handle first, after checking the safety. He took it, tossed it lightly in his hand to feel its heft, and nodded approvingly. He returned it to her, promising to gather a few larger pieces of artillery to leave with both Amy and Carey.

Matthews went outside to check the perimeter of the immediate property for any signs of where Mack may have headed, leaving Amy and Carey in the living room. "Well, well, 'Deputy' McDade…I like it," Carey teased before looking up at her shyly. "It's kind of…hot."

"How is 'Deputy McDade' hotter than 'Officer McDade'? I've been Officer McDade the whole time you had your tongue in my mouth, and it didn't seem to turn you on as much." She crossed her arms and gave him an icy stare, pretending to be insulted at her demotion.

"In my defense, you neglected to mention the part about being a cop for most of the time that said tongue was enjoying ravaging said mouth," he answered, looking smug. "In fact, I only found out about the cop part when you managed to get yourself pulled over for speeding."

"True, I'll own up to that," she casually replied, coming over to where Carey rested on the couch and stepping one foot over his legs, straddling him as she leaned over him. "But now, somehow, I'm 'hot' because I wear a uniform and carry a gun?"

"Nope." She raised an eyebrow at him suspiciously, staring him down as he answered. "You were already hot. The uniform just makes you *scorching*."

"You know, I've just been made a deputy in this county. I can put you in handcuffs," Amy said with a growl in her voice.

"I was really hoping you'd say that," Carey shot back, a wide-eyed expression on his face as he took her face in his hands and kissed her, mumbling something about having been a bad boy as their lips met. "But you didn't tell me the charge, *Deputy* McDade. Don't you have to tell me what I've done wrong?"

"You're guilty of wearing too many clothes, but tell me if I hurt you," she answered, taking her mouth from his as she nibbled her way down his neck, her fingers fumbling with the buttons on his shirt. He responded by grabbing her hips and pressing her against him, shrugging out of his shirt and being careful of his bandaged arm as Amy finished unbuttoning it.

Carey ran his fingertips under the hem of Amy's t-shirt, rubbing light circles against the overly warm skin of her back before sliding it upward, lifting her shirt off as she pulled her arms through. He took in the sight of her, her skin glistening in the faint glow of light that came from under the kitchen door. He ran his hands over the pink lace of her bra, watching her face as he took her perfect round breasts in his hands.

He let his hands move along the slope of her ribs and around to her back, about to reach for the clasp on her bra when a noise outside the door made them freeze. They looked first at each other and then at the door, before Amy pulled her gun and held it in one hand, deftly working her way back into the t-shirt Carey held out to her with her other hand.

She smoothed the fabric down on the front of her shirt just as Sheriff Matthews re-entered the house. He froze when he saw the gun in her hand, and looked somewhat confused that Carey was now shirtless, looking to each of them for an explanation.

"Sheriff," Carey began. "I'm sorry, we thought you left."

"Apparently," the grizzled, grey-haired lawman said with a knowing, amused look. "No, I was just checking the area outside the house for any sign of Mack but I didn't find anything. I don't think he's coming back around tonight, his little firebomb was probably all he had prepared. After all, if he thought everyone was asleep when he threw it, he probably assumed the rug would catch and send the whole house up in flames before anyone woke up enough to stop it. I bet we won't hear from him any more today, but I'd also bet you a good sized pile of money that he's probably hiding out and plotting his next move." The elderly sheriff walked to the door, his old injury causing him to limp in a more pronounced way than before. He turned and smiled with one hand on the doorknob. "Come lock up after me, and you two have a good day now, you hear?"

After he left and Amy turned the deadbolt, she returned to the couch to find Carey covering his face with his hands. "That was almost as bad as being walked in on by your parents...only instead, it was the cops! Why do I feel like a fifteen-year-old kid who was caught with his hand down someone's shirt in the movie theater?"

Amy couldn't help but laugh at the situation, covering her own embarrassment at the same time. "Oh, come on, it wasn't that bad. We're adults, not kids. And besides, we weren't really doing anything that embarrassing. It's not like he walked in right as you were throwing me down naked on the..." Her face froze, her last word hanging in mid-air. A horrified expression replaced her happy one.

"What? Amy, what is it?" Carey demanded, gripping both her wrists in his large hands.

"...the rug," she finished slowly, concentrating on her words. "Carey, is the sheriff a good friend of your family's? The kind of friend who would come out here a lot, stay for dinner, that kind of thing?"

Carey's confusion was hard to hide. "Not really. I mean, we've known him forever, but he has a lot of ground to cover and it's a pretty good trek to his office, practically across the county. We really only see him when we go into town. But what are you talking about? What's wrong with the rug?"

"Carey, he knew about the rug," she said, whispering as though Matthews was listening outside. "He knew that the bomb was supposed to land on the rug." She pointed with her hand to where the rug had been only an hour ago. "But we rolled it up and took it to the kitchen right after we put out the fire. It was already gone when he got here, so how did he know that Mack would try to catch the rug on fire? All Matthews was able to see was a gleaming wood floor, he wouldn't have known there used to be a rug here."

"I don't want to believe what I think you're saying," Carey said in a hushed tone, looking at the floor as though he could will it not to be true.

"The sheriff is in on it," Amy said quietly, visibly shrinking toward the safety of Carey's embrace. "That's how he knew where Mack intended to throw it. It's also the reason he hasn't been able to find Mack yet. It's because he doesn't want to."

Chapter Ten

"How many days out do you think we are from the auction in Missouri?" one of the vacationers asked Doug, a ranch hand, as they loaded gear for the day's trip.

"I wouldn't guess too much further, why? Aren't you having a good time?" he asked, genuinely interested in the fun-level of the drive. He looked at the small sea of faces and detected weariness, most likely from having spent the last week sleeping on the ground, only showering every second day, and using the finest bathrooms nature had to offer.

"Oh, no, it's not that," he replied. "This has been really amazing. We never see landscape like this back home, and the stars every night...well, they're just unbelievable. Yesterday's trip to the river gorge was really great." The man seemed a little too concerned with making Doug believe he was having a wonderful time, but his voice became lower as he continued, taking on a conspiratorial tone. "I just can't help but notice that people keep dropping off like flies. Are they okay?"

Doug smiled at the concerned man, truly appreciative that this city boy, who'd paid a hefty fee to play cowboy for a while, was actually worried about some of the Carsons and their team.

"Yeah, they're totally fine!" Doug promised, seeing a few of the faces start to relax a little. "You guys know we lost two of them right off the bat because they got married!" Some of the city people nodded with a smile at the memory of the impromptu wedding, while others who'd not known about it looked pleasantly puzzled. "And then we had two others head back to the ranch to take care of some unexpected business. It happens from time to time, and that's why we bring the vehicles and have so many of the hands help out. You know, those little things that come up, like a broken water main or something. Someone has to go back and sign off on repairs, be there to talk to a contractor, stuff like that, you know?"

The group seemed more at ease until Karen spoke up, barking at Doug in an angry voice. "Oh, really? So why did our little friend, Amy, have to leave? Is she suddenly a part of the Carson family, or let me guess...she's one of the contractors who's gonna fix the roof? Personally, I think your boy twisted her arm into going with him, probably told her all kinds of B.S. and made a bunch of promises that he doesn't intend to keep. We're gonna find her at the airport, used and discarded, and nursing a broken heart and wounded ego, aren't we?" Karen crossed her arms over her chest, her expression daring Doug to argue with her.

"No, ma'am, I promise you it's nothing like that," Doug answered kindly, sighing and forcing himself to not be rude. That was one of the old man's most important rules about the drive and the city people, no one was to ever be rude to their guests. "Ms. McDade was not actually enjoying her trip and she felt very out of her element. And, of course, getting injured by her horse spooked her a little bit, made her a little afraid of getting back in the saddle right away. When she found out Mr. Carson's son was headed back to the ranch, she asked to accompany him. I'm sure she's sitting on the porch right now, fanning herself from one of the old rocking chairs and having a nice glass of sweet tea."

Luckily for Doug, the group was more than a little tired of Karen's constant male bashing and militant complaining. They were all too happy to picture the scene he described, mostly to spite Karen. They grinned and went back to their chores, readying for another day of riding and leading the herd. He managed to fight the urge to mumble under his breath until he was well away from the group, rolling his eyes as he stomped back to where his own work awaited him, passing Bernard on his way.

"Good morning, sir, any news from back at the ranch?" He asked quietly and with a cheerful expression plastered on his face, not wanting to alert anyone that something was wrong at home and certainly not wanting to upset his boss.

"Not much," the man answered gruffly, keeping a tight lid on his updates from Carey and Anders. It was heartbreaking to him to even think about, but he'd grown wary of who he had working for him. Everywhere around him, he saw people he thought he knew, people he'd worked with for years. Now that he knew the truth about some of them, he couldn't risk so much as a comforting word for fear that his words would be used against his family. Bernard had no idea who he could trust at the moment. "But they're back at the ranch and seem to have everything under control. I hope I didn't make it seem worse than it was, just needed Carey to head back and help Anders. You know how his asthma is at this time of year…" He left his weak excuse hanging between them before turning and walking away, leaving Doug to stare after him in confusion.

The drovers and their guests headed out for the day, watching carefully as most of the day's route would take the cattle along and across paved highways and trafficked two-lane roads. The opportunity for a large vehicle to spook the cattle and cause a stampede was pretty great, so the ranch hands scattered themselves more along the flank of the herd and stayed in and among the city people.

"Dwayne, come in," a squawking metallic voice said to the foreman over the radio.

"This is Dwayne, go ahead," he answered, speaking into his earpiece's oval microphone clipped to his shirt collar.

"I'm afraid it looks like we won't be at the midday meet-up point, we have a flat tire on the truck."

Dwayne swore under his breath, fighting to keep a pleasant look on his face. "What happened? I just had new tires put on the truck the week before we left! I bought them specifically for the drive! Did you run over something? A nail or anything like that?"

"Negative. It just went flat." Static crackled through the voiceless radio. "We'll get a tow in here to fix it, but we won't see you guys before tonight."

Dwayne looked around in frustration and caught Joseph's eye. The younger Carson boy steered his horse in the foreman's direction and came up beside him. "What's going on?"

He explained to Joseph in a hushed voice about the tire, looking around to see if anyone had noticed his angry muttering.

"And you're thinking it's sabotage because a vehicle that drove on a major highway had a flat tire?" Joseph teased, a mischievous glint in his hazel eyes.

"I'm telling you, Joseph, someone is messing around with us. First, we have that problem with the water tank on the support vehicle, and no one can get a shower. Then, the propane hose on the food truck splits and there's no way to cook the food. Now this. I don't like it, not at all."

"Is it possible all those things are just coincidences? Any of those problems could have happened back on the ranch, right?" Joseph asked, looking to Dwayne to confirm that his fears were unfounded.

"Sure, they could. But all three of them happening this week? I don't like it, especially not with what's happening back home. Think about it, that propane hose could have blown us all up if that's what someone was going for." Dwayne kept his eyes open for wandering cattle and eavesdropping ears.

"You can't really think that Mack has followed us up here," Joseph said with a derisive laugh, trying to point out how ridiculous that would have to be.

"Not for a second. But he could have someone who was already on the drive who's setting us up." Both cowboys looked around nervously for a second, eyeing the other drovers and the vacationers with suspicion.

"No," Joseph finally argued. "there's no way any of these guys could be out to get us. I mean, come on, really, I've known all these guys my whole life! And these new people, don't get me wrong but I'm not sure they'd know how to cut a propane line! Or what propane is for!"

"I want to believe you and say you're completely right, but I just have this nagging feeling that something else is going on. I wish I could shake it, I really do. It's ruining this whole drive for me. I can't even enjoy this part of the job, all I can think about is getting back home in one piece and making sure Amanda's okay." Dwayne looked around with a mixture of apprehension and sadness, watching the faces of each character within his sight.

"It's gonna be fine, you'll see," the younger cowboy promised, before giving his reins a flick and nudging his horse back toward his position. "If it gets to be too much, just tell Dad how you feel. I'm sure the last thing he'd do is make you stay on up here if you really thought your wife was in danger. You know he thinks of all of you like family."

Dwayne nodded morosely and spit out the toothpick he'd been nervously chewing on since breakfast, barely mustering up the energy to wave his hand to Joseph as he left. He realized he was spending as much time watching his co-workers as he was watching his cows, so much that he wondered if he'd actually lost half the herd when he wasn't paying attention.

Little did he know, he'd get his wish to return to the ranch sooner rather than later. Within the hour, an older calf took off at a dead run away from the herd, heading out into a scraggly patch of dirt and scrub. With a loud, excited yell, Joseph took off after it, kicking his horse lightly to make it give chase, his hat flying off and catching to hang down his back by its leather chord.

The vacationers all turned to watch Joseph rope this calf and bring it back to the group, appreciative of seeing some real cowboy action instead of just staged rope tricks for their amusement. He veered to the animal's right side to come at it from an angle, chasing it when it suddenly changed direction in its confusion.

As they watched in awe, his horse took off after the surprisingly fast calf, dirt from the two animals' hooves kicking up in clouds as they ran and maneuvered. Finally, the calf turned back in the direction of the herd and sped up, eager to put his brief adventure behind him. Joseph's horse stayed close enough on the calf's heels to keep the smaller animal headed in the right direction but suddenly, his horse stopped short, sending Joseph flying over its head and crashing to the rocky ground with a sickening thud.

"Doug!" Dwayne yelled into his radio mic before kicking his own horse into action. He reached Joseph just as the other man's voice answered on the radio. "Joseph's been thrown, get the other hands to even out the line while I see how bad off he is."

Dwayne hopped out of his saddle and came over to kneel by Joseph's head, relieved that at least the boy's eyes were open. Joseph had a hand clutching his shoulder, his face a mask of pain. He moaned loudly as he moved from side to side, wincing and grimacing as waves of pain radiated through his chest.

"Okay, now. Hold still. Let's see how bad it is. Looks like maybe you have…oh, shit, that's gross. Dude, your collarbone is sticking up through your skin! Don't touch it!" Dwayne commanded, pulling Joseph's arm away from the spot where he wanted to clutch the pain. "It's open, you're going to get dirt in it. Look at me, no, open your eyes and let me see your pupils."

Joseph finally did as he was told, letting his unfocused eyes come to rest somewhere near Dwayne's face and grinning foolishly. "Betcha think this is Crazy Mack's fault, too, huh?"

Dwayne laughed at his own fears from earlier. "Well, it's not entirely impossible. He could have released a snake in front of your horse or something. He could have planted a microchip in your horse's ear that makes an awful sound and spooks it. He could have…"

"…and I could have been riding the dumbest horse we own. He probably saw his own shadow and decided to let that other horse go in front of him." Joseph closed his eyes as the pain burned through his shoulder.

Word had gotten back to Bernard in the RV and his desperate voice called through the radio for an update. Dwayne spoke into his microphone and let him know they needed to halt the drive until medical help came, then switched his attention to giving orders to the ranch hands. "Luckily, we're on pavement today, so call an ambulance and we'll wait here. Go ahead and tell the others to put out some feed for the herd and get the water tanker up here to water them."

He looked up in time to see an older woman walking toward him gingerly, picking her way through the scrub and stickers to get there. Sandra, one of the vacationers, approached and smiled. "Hi! I'm a retired nurse, can I do anything?"

"Be my guest, ma'am. It's pretty obvious his collarbone's broken, but it's his head I'm worried about. He's got the trademark Carson hard head, but this might have been too much for even his skull to take," Dwayne said lightly, trying to keep from upsetting the older woman.

"Oh, it's not his collarbone I'm worried about," Sandra said lightly, opening Joseph's shirt with her wrinkled, knobby fingers. "It's this right here." She pointed to an angry red patch on his side where a nasty bruise was already forming. "You might have yourself some broken ribs, young man."

Sandra leaned her ear down directly to Joseph's chest and listened. "Sorry for getting in your personal space here a bit, but I didn't bring a stethoscope! Just bear with me." She listened for a time, trying not to smoosh Joseph any more than absolutely necessary. "It's just as I thought. I hear a really 'wet' sound in there, it's possible one of his ribs has punctured his lung."

"Oh my God!" Dwayne shouted, crouching back down next to Joseph protectively. "What do we do?"

"Well, we're already doing it. We wait for the ambulance," she said with a kind smile. "We'll just need to let them know that when they arrive."

After what seemed like well over an hour, an ambulance finally pulled around the bend in the highway and slowed down as it rolled to the edge of the shoulder. It slowly bounced along the rough dirt until it came to a stop nearby, sending even more dust up in the air. The paramedics jumped out and got to work, assessing Joseph's injuries and taking his information.

Finally, they thought they could move him, and proceeded to pack Joseph up on a gurney and put him in the back of the vehicle. The crew drove away slowly until they hit the pavement, Bernard promising to intercept them and follow them to the hospital when he called through the radio.

"Dwayne, I need you to take charge of the drive. You know the route, and you can radio me if there are any questions, anything at all. Understood?" Bernard squeaked through the radio. Dwayne closed his eyes and thought for a moment, taking deep breaths.

"Are you sure we shouldn't just call it off, sir? We can find a local farm to let the cattle graze until we can get some trucks in here. With you, Casey, Carey, and now Joseph off the drive, there's no one from Carson Hill except the two younger twins. Wouldn't you feel better waiting until someone else can join us?"

It was quiet for a moment, so long that Dwayne thought maybe Bernard had cut off his radio, ready to fly after the ambulance carrying his son. Finally, his voice came through the speaker. "Just keep moving, keep a slow pace. I'll try to contact someone from the ranch and see if I can get them to join you. And, Dwayne,...please be careful."

Chapter Eleven

"NO!" The younger girl screamed, throwing a wooden chair in the direction of the older woman holding out the spoon. "I don't want that crap! I want FOOD! Real food! I'm outta here!" Emma bolted for the door, enraged when she figured out for the hundredth time that she was locked in. "Let! Me! OUT!"

The kind woman simply watched Emma's antics, her expression remaining completely impassive. She didn't reinforce the girls' outbursts by trying to talk to them in this state, but she didn't react to them either. Years of training and experience had taught her how to handle someone coming off a meth addiction, but every single addict was different and suffered in her own way.

"Emma, I promise you'll feel better if you get some food in you," the farm's teacher, Ms. Crane, began in a calm, level voice, still holding out the spoon and bowl. She flinched only slightly when Emma stomped toward her and knocked the bowl out of her hands, sending cream of wheat splattering across the floor and up the wall of the cabin. "That isn't necessary. Remember to speak to me with words if you need to tell me something."

Ms. Crane picked up a chair that had been kicked over and righted it at the table before sitting in it. She reached for the deck of cards from the middle of the rough wooden table and began shuffling them idly, doing her best to ignore Emma's screams. The girl was so skinny even when she first showed up, and a week and a half of trying to fight the effects of the drug that had invaded practically every cell in her body had left her emaciated and scabbed.

"I don't have to use my words!" Emma screamed in the woman's ear, slapping at the teacher's hands and scattering the cards in every direction. Ms. Crane sighed, then wordlessly stood up and crossed the large single room to sit on the overstuffed sofa, picking up a magazine and flipping through the pages without looking at Emma.

"Emma, I understand you're suffering and I know you will be very sad when you find out that you've slapped me. For now, remember to keep your hands to yourself. If you need to hit something, remember what I've told you: you may hit the couch cushions." Ms. Crane pointed to the end of the sofa, which had already been pummeled to the point of lumpiness.

Ms. Crane couldn't help but notice that Dee was still curled up in a ball on the floor, her face resting against the cool surface of the hardwood floor. She'd stayed there most of yesterday and all through the night, not even letting the older woman cover her with a blanket or wipe at her damp forehead, screaming in actual pain at the slightest touch on her skin. She had been so eerily quiet through her ordeal, Ms. Crane had to keep fighting the urge to check her pulse, mostly because she was afraid of what she might find.

Both girls had been as wretched looking as drowned kittens when she took them from the Carson Hill main house to this cabin some miles away. Mr. Carson had only just bought this smaller ranch at auction, intending to give it to his new daughter-in-law as a wedding present, and it was lucky he did. When Dee and Emma had shown up on the Carson's ranch one day, there was no way they could go back to town, not after what they'd suffered at the hands of Crazy Mack. When the drugs left their system and they finally began the healing process, they both would face years of therapy to help them overcome the horrors he'd put them through, first getting them addicted and then using that very drug to make them complacent as he prostituted them.

Now, they both alternated between screaming and writhing, with periods of unnerving silence in between. Luckily, at least so far, they had stuck to an impromptu schedule of alternating for Ms.

Crane so that they weren't both screaming at the same time. *Thank goodness for small favors*, Ms. Crane thought to herself sourly. *I don't know if I could handle both of them freaking out at once. This is why I left teen rehab behind.*

"He's coming for us," a small voice said during a lull in Emma's screaming. Ms. Crane immediately jumped up and ran to crouch beside Dee on the floor.

"What? What did you say, dear?" The woman asked, smoothing the sweaty hair back from where it was plastered to the girl's clammy forehead.

"He's coming for us. He'll find us and he'll kill us."

"No, sweetie, Mack isn't going to hurt you. I promise. I won't let him hurt you."

"He'll kill us," Dee repeated quietly, her eyes not moving from the spot on the wall where they'd stared for hours. "He said so. He said he'd kill us if we ever left."

Ms. Crane sighed, closing her eyes and willing God to give her the words to say that would comfort this poor girl. Even she was surprised at what came out of her mouth.

"No, sweetie. He won't hurt you, and that is my promise. I swear to you, I'll kill him first myself." Ms. Crane gave Dee a determined, confident smile and patted the girl's hand firmly. She pushed herself up off the floor and was relieved to see that Emma had pretty much burned herself out and was now lying on the floor across the room from her friend. The two girls reminded the teacher of paper dolls, thrown to the ground after their owner tired of playing with them.

Ms. Crane breathed a sigh of relief and went to get some rest herself, settling on the sofa after checking the locks on the doors and each window one more time. Something about Dee's haunting, hollow voice had her spooked too, or maybe it was just the way the girl seemed so calm, so resigned to what she thought would happen to them. Covering each girl with a blanket before turning in herself, she decided to keep one small lamp burning and her hand on the semi-automatic handgun Mr. Carson had armed her with before sending her on this lonely adventure.

Everyone says things will look brighter in the morning, but someone forgot to tell Dee and Emma. Dee was still curled in a ball and Ms. Crane's mind went immediately to the possible shutdown of her kidneys, given that she hadn't had to get up to go to the bathroom in almost forty-eight hours. The girl hadn't been able to eat or drink anything in that time, either, but that shouldn't have done it.

"Dee, sweetie, you have to get up," the teacher began, shaking the girl awake and feeling flooded with relief when she opened her eyes slightly. "Come on, you rested all day yesterday. I'm sorry, but you have to get up and move today." She put her hands under Dee's arms and began to lift her, horrified that the girl weighed almost nothing.

Dee didn't fight her, but she didn't help support her weight either. She hung limply in Ms. Crane's arms, too weak from the exhaustion and lack of food to do anything more than be carried. After she managed to get Dee cleaned up and in the bed, Ms. Crane turned her attention to Emma, who was lying in the floor next to a small puddle of her own vomit. She carried Emma next, cleaning her up and putting her in the bed with Dee.

Ms. Crane returned to the small kitchen and got to work making a thin broth, peeling a pot full of potatoes and putting them on to boil to mash into the broth when the girls felt like eating something again. She made sure there was plenty of bottled water in the fridge, and filled a kettle with cold water and tea bags so it would be ready to make sweet tea when the girls felt like drinking something.

After finishing the random chores and cleaning up a little bit around the cabin, she checked on the sleeping girls once more before returning to her chair in the front room. From her chair, she watched out the window for any signs of Mack, all the while keeping a pistol close to her side.

Chapter Twelve

Miranda pulled her cowboy hat further down over her eyes to block the bright sunlight that was intruding on her nap. She'd spent the last week lounging in a chaise beside the hotel pool with Casey, when the two of them hadn't felt the need to head back up to their room for a while, that is. Ordering in from room service and alternating between the oversized chaise and the bed had left her dreamily lazy and completely blissful.

Casey lounged next to her, his fingers interlaced with hers. He ran his fingertips idly over the heavy wedding band and engagement ring that he'd only put there a matter of days ago. "Yeah, I'm still getting used to that myself," Miranda said sleepily without opening her eyes, a smile playing across her full lips.

"And I'm getting used to seeing you with clothes on again," he said in a husky whisper, bringing her hand to his lips and kissing her palm, then placing light kisses on each of her fingertips.

"Seriously? This swim suit is the most clothing I've had on all week!" she said with a laugh. "And even this wouldn't count as covered enough to even go into a convenience store!" Casey smiled at the truth, rolling toward her on the double chaise and pulling her closer to him, turning her so that they both lay on their sides.

"I happen to be incredibly fond of that swimsuit," he replied, working one finger under the single string that held her top in place, teasing the skin along her back until he made his way around to her side, barely grazing the sensitive skin along her breast until she shivered. "Remember to turn us so we don't tan like this!" Casey mumbled in her ear in a sleepy, satisfied voice, letting her know that he had no intention of moving soon. Somewhere behind him, his phone buzzed on the table, pinging that he'd received a text. He didn't release his grip on Miranda by even a fraction, happily ignoring the intrusion.

"Sweetie, aren't you going to pick that up?" She asked keeping her eyes closed as she threw her hat down on the stone patio beside her.

"Nope." He hugged her even closer to him.

"Casey Carson! It could be Gracie! Please?" She asked, reminding him that her baby sister was without her only family member on the cattle drive.

"It can't possibly be Gracie. Her fingers had to have fallen off by now from all the texts she's sent you! She'd have to be texting with her toes!"

"First of all, I'm sure she *can* text with her feet...she's thirteen! And remember, I warned you that she'd do this. I'm the only family she has and she's never been alone before."

"I'm only teasing, honey, I knew she was part of the package when I married you. And my whole family is better off for it, for having both of you." He kissed her firmly on the cheek, but pulled away to pick up his phone like she'd asked. He held it up and pressed the screen, jolting upright after reading the message for only a few seconds. Miranda sat up in alarm, grabbing Casey's arm as she spoke.

"What is it, sweetie? Is it Gracie?" Casey shook his head silently, his brow creasing as he continued reading. "Oh, God, is it your dad?"

"No, nothing like that. Don't worry. I just have to call them." He got up off the lounge chair to make a phone call but Miranda stopped him and pulled him back, sitting him down beside her and taking his face between her hands. She looked at his eyes intensely, determination in her tone of voice.

"Casey Carson, do not walk away from me. Whatever business you have back home involves me now, too. We don't shield anything from each other, and we don't keep secrets. I'm a Carson now, too…remember?"

Casey closed his eyes and leaned his forehead against hers for a moment. He nodded. "I'm sorry, you're completely right. This is so new to me, too. I just wanted to protect you."

"Protect me from what? What's wrong?" she pleaded, taking his hands.

"There's a problem back at the ranch. Don't worry, Gracie's fine," he said, putting a finger to Miranda's lips when she started to interrupt so he could read the series of text messages that continued to cause his phone to beep. "She's still on the drive. But Carey's at the house for some reason and he's been hurt, and Joseph is on his way to the hospital. Dad's meeting him there. Apparently…Crazy Mack came around, causing problems and making all kinds of threats. He's the reason Carey's injured."

"Oh, no! What do we need to do?" she asked, searching Casey's face.

"I'm so sorry to ask you this, but would it be horrible to cut our honeymoon a little short? I promise, when the drive is over and everyone's safe, we'll pick right up where we left off."

"Of course, Casey! Anywhere you are *is* my honeymoon, for the rest of our lives, and I don't care whether it's a fancy resort or a cow pasture. But you know that family comes first. Where should we go, home or to meet up with the drive?" Miranda was already gathering her towel and sunscreen, ready to head to the room and pack up.

"Well, I'm sure my dad will head back to the ranch once Joseph's released from the hospital. And you know…I'm sorry to tell you this…but Gracie's still with the drive and there's no one from the family there with her." Miranda's eyes widened in shock, "Wait, I promise she's in good hands, those people might as well be our family. But I know you'd feel better if we were with her. I would too."

Miranda nodded, exhaling a breath she hadn't realized she'd been holding. "You're right. Let me go get my boots on, cowboy, we got us a cattle drive to get to!" she said with a nervous smile. Casey pulled her into a tight embrace and kissed her passionately, oblivious to anyone who might see them. *Let them look, I'm the luckiest man alive*, he thought as he deepened their kiss.

They walked hand in hand to the bank of elevators that led to the suites, feeling the disappointment of cutting their time together short but knowing that they had obligations that wouldn't wait. If they hurried, they could be on the road within the hour, and make the four-hour drive to rendezvous with the group by nightfall.

Chapter Thirteen

Amy and Carey stood post at two different windows on opposite ends of the first floor, staring out into the darkness for Mack or any of the faceless and possibly unlimited number of people who could be working with him. His burns still wrapped in gauze and still excruciating, Carey didn't trust himself with a loaded gun, not when he still needed so much pain medicine. Instead, he kept watch, ready to alert Amy if anything looked strange. He also had a radio connecting him to Anders and to Amy, but they'd agreed not to use it until they had to so anyone lurking outside wouldn't know their whereabouts.

They had spent the whole day converting the kitchen into a safe zone, moving enough beds for the remaining house staff into the large, windowless room. It was pure luck that they had plenty of bottled water and prepared food in the supply room, because Mack, or someone working for him, had cut the wires to the house, leaving them without electricity. As Anders had realized that first day when they huddled in fear, the large industrial refrigerators provided an added layer of protection if bullets started flying, even if they no longer kept their food from spoiling.

It was Anders who thought of also cutting the gas to the three oversized six-burner stoves, just in case Mack tried anything that could cause an explosion. And Amy had been the one to reject the high-powered rifle and ammo the sheriff had left them in case it was intentionally ineffective, helping herself to the store of the Carson's small artillery instead.

That left Carey feeling pretty much useless, and missing his twin brother even more. Casey would have taken charge from the very beginning, and would probably have caught Mack that first night. He also wouldn't have been stupid enough to bring the sheriff out here when he was in on it the whole time. Carey felt more lost than ever without his twin.

Wait a minute, Carey thought to himself in shock, sitting up so suddenly that pain shot through the damaged nerve endings in his heat-seared skin. *This isn't about those two girls. It might have been at first, but not anymore.* He picked up his handheld radio and brought it close to his mouth and spoke in a low voice.

"Amy, come in," Carey said quietly, waiting with his fingers on the volume knob, ready to dial it down in a hurry if her response was too sharp. She took the hint from his whispered transmission and responded by simply pressing her transmit button without saying a word.

"I think I know what's going on. Mack wants his two cash cows back; sure, I'll believe that. But why would the sheriff help Mack with his little prostitution ring? He might look the other way, especially if his deputies, or heck, even the sheriff himself, had spent some after-hours time at the bar. But to come out here and know that Mack was going to try to burn us out? That would have been almost a dozen counts of murder if Mack's plan had succeeded. You don't take a chance on killing people, accidentally or not, over a couple of runaway prostitutes. There has to be more to this than that."

"What else are you thinking it could it be?" Amy whispered into her radio, suddenly very business-like. Carey could almost see her face in his mind, her forehead creased with worry, her blue eyes practically burning as she thought over what he would say next. He pushed aside the thoughts of her beautiful features and answered her.

Carey's anger at his own understanding of the situation made him no longer concerned about secrecy and silence. "Those two showed up here looking like the most pathetic, half-starved, half-dead, and half-alive creatures I've ever laid eyes on. They were so strung out on drugs, it's a wonder they could even walk on their little stick legs, let alone find the place. My dad put them up in a cabin off our property so they could clean up a little before we helped them figure out what to do next."

"It's not uncommon for prostitutes to use drugs, Carey." She knew from her several years' experience on the street and had always felt some level of empathy for those working women—many of them just kids, while just as many of them were hardened, older women—who'd ended up in prostitution and drugs, because it was often hard to tell which had come first in their lives.

"Yeah, but where'd they get the drugs? Even the sheriff said Mack was suspected of selling drugs. He's been doping those girls up and pimping them out with the same stuff he sells. And the sheriff's getting paid to look the other way, if he's not actually a part of the operation."

"And you think Mack isn't worried so much about getting his hookers back as he is getting his witnesses back," Amy stated boldly, her voice beginning to shake with anger as she put it all together.

"Exactly. By the time he fed them, clothed them, and kept them pumped full of drugs, he couldn't have been making that much money off them. They were just another draw to get guys in the door of his bar. But now that they're gone, he has no way of knowing what they'll say and who they'll say it to."

"But for the sheriff to put himself at this much risk, he has to be in pretty deep. And those girls must have seen him," Amy said angrily. There were a lot of things she could tolerate, but a crooked cop was not one of them.

Carey felt anxious. A part of him was kind of hoping that Amy, with her years of police training, would shoot his theory full of holes and tell him it just wasn't possible. He'd been counting on her to come up with a different idea, one that was safer and meant that the police and a drug dealer weren't outside at that very moment, ready to stop at nothing to protect their business and their secret.

At the same time, it felt good to be believed and to finally make sense of what was happening. His contentment was short-lived when Amy's voice came through the radio again.

"I know you don't want to scare your dad, especially with your brother in the hospital, but this is now officially bigger than both of us. We need to get on the satellite phone and have him radio the DEA. We need some armed officials we can trust, not any of these local or even nearby state guys. There's no telling how far Matthews' reach spreads."

Carey held his radio up to answer, but never had the chance. He felt the dull blow of a solid object colliding with the back of his head, momentarily blinded by bright flashes of radiating pain behind his eyes. His knees gave way underneath him and he crumpled to the floor, landing facedown and unconscious.

Chapter Fourteen

"Miranda!" Gracie screamed in excitement, flying at her older sister and tackling her in a hug. "I'm so glad you're back! Did you have a good honeymoon? Was it...*romantic?*" she asked, batting her eyelashes and pretending to swoon.

"I'm not answering that until you are much, much older," Miranda answered with a shocked laugh. She was most surprised by the change in Gracie's whole personality, for the better of course. The mousy girl who'd been through one horrible ordeal after another in her short life had been replaced by this exuberant, bouncy cowgirl. *We'll live on this cattle drive year-round for all I care, if it will keep that smile on Gracie's face,* She thought. "Have you had a good time? Did you behave yourself?"

"Yes, and yes," Gracie answered soundly with a firm nod. She grinned broadly, lighting up her sun-kissed face. "So are you guys gonna finish the drive with us?"

"That we are! We're here 'til the end of the line!" Casey said, coming up behind Miranda and pulling her in a passionate hug that made Gracie stick her tongue out.

"Ewwwww, it's not gonna be like that the whole rest of the trip, is it? They only feed us so many meals a day, and if I puke..."

"We promise to behave ourselves," Miranda promised with a sly smile. "At least when impressionable children are around! Weren't you the one who was just asking me for juicy details?" Casey stiffened behind her, the look of embarrassed horror on his face enough to send Gracie into fits of giggles.

"I'm out! Girl talk can commence upon my departure!" He walked away with a wave behind him, headed off to check on their horses and to load their gear for the ride. Gracie turned to her older sister with a serious look.

"Miranda, are you really happy?" She asked, cringing a little bit. "I mean, I know you only came out here because of me, because of what…that guy…did to me." Miranda didn't need any reminders of finding her drunken ex-boyfriend trying to force himself on her little sister, because the memory of that image would be burned in her brain until the day she died. She took both of Gracie's hands in hers and beamed.

"Gracie, we didn't come out west because of you. We came because we both needed a fresh start and a new outlook on life. But to answer your question, yes, I'm one hundred percent, ecstatically happy!" Miranda pulled her baby sister into a hug and held her, rubbing small, reassuring circles on her back. When they stepped apart, there were tears in the big sister's eyes, brilliant happiness showing in the younger.

"Ready to go?" Gracie asked, eager to get back on her beloved horse and keep moving. This whole experience had been less about empowering her and more about just letting her be a typical teenage girl who loved horses. So what if she'd been sleeping on the ground and eating her food off her lap? It was a small price to pay for this kind of freedom.

They walked arm in arm to the temporary corral to saddle up, Miranda telling Gracie the limited details about where they went, how nice the hotel had been, and other harmless specifics like that. Gracie shared the news from the drive, that first Carey had gone back home to look after the ranch because of some problem—she didn't know what—and then Joseph had been taken to the hospital after being thrown from his horse, meaning Bernard had gone with him.

"I thought all this only happened yesterday! So you've been here alone this whole time?" Miranda shrieked before lowering her voice.

"Puh-lease," Gracie answered, rolling her eyes. "You call this alone? There's, like, forty people running around!"

"But none of them were part of the family! We left you with strangers!" Miranda's expression turned from shocked to horrified as her mind raced with the possibilities of everything that could have gone wrong.

"No, silly, I stayed with Emily the whole time. I was fine!" Gracie beamed proudly. "Besides, you needed to get away. You've been taking care of me for so long that you probably forgot how to be a regular person."

Miranda was somewhat relieved when she remembered that the Carson's head cook, Emily, had promised to take care of Gracie, but her heart still raced at the thought of her little sister traveling halfway across the country without so much as a distant cousin she was related to.

"Well, I'm here now. And I'll be sure not to abandon you again," Miranda said in a serious voice.

"Oh, goody. You're not going to turn all-weird and possessive, are you? I mean, you'll want to spend some time with your new husband, right?" Gracie hinted, her own fears of being smothered and mollycoddled showing through.

"Nice try, kiddo. There's time for 'spending time with my new husband' when we're all safely back home. And to answer your question, yes, as a matter of fact, I am going to be all weirdly protective." The look of surprise on Gracie's face made Miranda laugh. "Yeah, mind reading is this skill adults develop when they suddenly find themselves in charge of teenage girls! Come on, let's get going."

They climbed up on their horses after checking that their carry bags were strapped firmly in place behind their saddles, and then followed the line of cowboys and temporary ranchers away from the campsite. As they helped guide the herd along winding trails, Miranda couldn't help but feel a small sense of connection to the generations who'd done this for hundreds of years, knowing that for many of those years, it was Carson ancestors who led their herds to market across an open, dangerous landscape. It made her appreciate Bernard all over again, first that he chose to conduct his farm in the old ways but also for his conniving interference that had brought her here. She said a quick prayer of gratitude for the old man and for his entire family, especially her new husband.

A husband! She thought to herself, her breath hitching for only a second. *Oh my God, I'm married.* A smile of blissful disbelief broke out across her face and she looked down so no one would catch her giddy expression. But one person saw her before she could turn away.

"Whatcha smiling about, wife?" Casey asked teasingly, bringing his horse up beside hers. "From the looks of that gorgeous smile, it's something good!"

"Oh, it is. It's very good," she said, meeting his gaze with a knowing look. "I was actually just thinking about you, and I couldn't help myself. Realizing for a second that this is real and that we're really married just made me smile for some reason."

Casey reached over and took her hand, bringing it to his lips and kissing her warmly before looking at her with a serious expression. "*You* make me smile, for every reason. I love you, Miranda."

She grinned again and blew him a kiss before answering, "I love you, too." He gave her his best heart stopping smile and kicked his horse forward, rejoining the lead riders who would watch out for the herd. Beside her, Gracie made obnoxious gagging noises at their sappy display. Miranda couldn't help but laugh. "Just wait, missy, you'll know what this feels like someday!"

"I can only hope," the girl said with a sigh. "But I'm looking around and seeing nothing but cows. You know I really do love it here, but how am I supposed to go on dates or go to my prom and do normal kid things like that? There's not even a mall here!"

"Luckily for both of us, we have a few years until finding your soulmate is an appropriate cause for concern! But I know what you mean about a social life, I've been a little worried about that, too. I want you to have a normal life, so we'll just have to work together to come up with what 'normal' means around here. In the meantime, there's school and work on the ranch. I mean, it's not like there aren't any kids close to your age."

"I know," Gracie said, trying really hard not to whine. "But there aren't any girls. Who am I supposed to swap secret crush stories with, and talk about hair and clothes? The *boys*? Give me a break!" Her good mood was gone, just like that, replaced by slumped shoulders and a self-pitying scowl.

"Gracie, I promise it'll be okay. We'll just have to take lots of trips to do our shopping and socializing, and you'll make friends online. Have you even checked in with your friends back home?"

"What's the point? It's not like I can invite them over for a 'spend the night' party," she answered grumpily. "Besides, what would I tell them? 'Hey! Guess what I did today? I brushed a horse and chased some cows! Yeah, I know I totally did that yesterday, but now it's today!' No, thanks."

Miranda was quiet for a minute as they rode along, the two of them shouldering some members of the herd back in line with their mounts. She couldn't be sure how much of Gracie's attitude was from being left alone while she went on her honeymoon, and how much was from genuinely missing out on some of the normal teenage things she should be doing at her age.

"Do you want us to leave?" She asked her sister quietly. Her heart almost stopped when Gracie didn't answer right away, afraid that she was going to have to make a costly decision where her sister was concerned.

"No," she finally answered. "I really wish I could stay here forever. I just want to have both worlds, one where there's normal stuff happening, and one where I get to live at the ranch. I know it's not possible, so it just makes me frustrated." Gracie blew her hair out of her eyes with an angry sigh.

"Are you sure? This isn't about anything else, is it?" She asked, ducking down to meet her sister's eye.

"Like what?" Gracie asked, looking up in confusion.

"Well...you're sure it's not about me suddenly being a member of their family and making you feel like an outsider, is it?" Miranda asked, genuinely worried about how her sister would feel as the outsider on the ranch, not exactly part of the nuclear family, and not part of the beloved staff.

"No! Everyone's been super nice, whether I'm family or not!" The girl insisted.

"Oh, sweetie, that's the thing...you *are* family! The day I married Casey, I became a Carson. That makes you their sister-in-law. You went from having no one in the world but me, to having a huge family, all when I said, 'I do'. You're not an outsider!"

Gracie didn't look convinced. She stared down at her hands, where they sat folded on her saddle horn, watching them move on their own as her horse swayed side to side. "Where am I going to live?" She whispered softly, a tear sliding down her cheek and splashing on her pants leg.

"What do you mean?" Miranda asked in surprise, reaching over and lifting the front of Gracie's hat to see her face.

"When you and Casey go live in your little love nest, where am I supposed to go? I can't go with you because I'd just be in the way. Am I supposed to just stay at the Carson's ranch with

106

strangers?" Her lower lip trembled in a way that broke Miranda's heart.

"You are *never* in the way, Gracie! You and I are a package deal, and I made sure the Carsons knew it before we ever set foot on that bus. And everyone here adores you. Did you know that they used to have a baby sister?" Gracie looked at her sister in shock before shaking her head, her curls flying out at angles from her hat. "She died at birth. That's when they lost their mom. They didn't just lose the best mother anyone ever had; they lost their sister, too. You're their chance to have a little sister again, and they know it."

"They didn't lose the best mother in the world...I did." It was Miranda's turn to stare, open-mouthed and dumbfounded, at her sister's words. Gracie never talked about their mother, especially not about the day she'd come home from school and found their mother dead of a heart attack on the living room floor. "Mom was the best. She was perfect."

Miranda reached her hand out and took her sister's fingers in her own, giving them a loving squeeze and letting Gracie just talk. The girl spoke, at last. About the things she'd kept buried inside for the past year, building up to the moment of truth: she'd fought with her mother the last time they'd spoken.

"I said evil, hurtful, horrible things to her before I left for school that morning," Gracie said, a fresh set of tears spilling from her sad eyes. "I told her I wished I didn't have to live there anymore, that I wanted...that I wanted to live with you." She buried her head on her sister's shoulder as she spoke, releasing the secret guilt she'd carried all alone since her mother's death.

"Gracie, I know. Mom called me after you left for school that morning. She told me about your argument and even asked if you could stay with me for a little while."

"She was actually going to kick me out?" Gracie cried in alarm.

"No, no! She was trying to give you what you wanted! She thought maybe you needed a little time away, some time to go be a big girl with her older sister, that's all. She only meant for the Christmas holidays, because my office closed when the boss' kids were out of school.

"But, honey, not once did she ever sound upset or angry, or sound like she didn't love you. She adored you, and lived her whole life for you. Nothing you could have ever said or done would change that."

Gracie wiped her nose on the thin cotton sleeve of her shirt, nodding thoughtfully. "I think, deep down, I knew that but I kept it right underneath the feeling that I made her have that heart attack when I was so horrible to her."

"Gracie…sweetie…it doesn't work that way. You didn't do that. And Mom would certainly not want you to beat yourself up all the time. You're an amazing, wonderful girl, and I'm proud you're my sister. And the Carsons are proud to know you, too. It's all going to be okay, you'll see!"

"Promise?" Gracie asked with a residual sniffle.

"I promise."

"Pinkie promise?"

"One hundred percent. Both pinkies, even," Miranda answered with a supportive smile. She tugged on her sister's stray curls and leaned over slightly in her saddle so she could link her arm through Gracie's. She let Gracie fill her in on everything she'd missed on the drive, and then answered a few questions about what their plans were now that she and Casey were back home.

Home, Miranda thought as Gracie rambled on. *It certainly means something different for me now than it used to.* She, too, had lost her mom, even if the pain of that loss wasn't as sharp as it was for Gracie. Miranda had been out on her own and on her own two feet for a few years when Mom had died, but Gracie was still so young that she needed a mother. Miranda had tried her best to make a home for Gracie, but it was a pathetic home at best.

Now, she and Gracie had their best chance in years to be a part of a real family, one where different people came in and out all day long, laughing and supporting each other. Loving her very own rugged cowboy was just an added benefit to being a part of this family.

Miranda spotted Casey up ahead and admired the effortless way he rode, as though being a cowboy was so much a part of him that it was impossible to separate it from him. Her heart thudded in her chest when she realized he was checking on his wife—*oh my God, I'm his wife,* she remembered for the hundredth time—as he turned in his saddle and looked back in her direction, giving her a thumbs up sign to see if she was okay back there.

I can't believe it, she thought, an involuntary, giddy smile breaking out on her face. *This is real. He's really mine…*

Chapter Fifteen

Somewhere in the fog, Carey could hear a voice, and it was laughing.

It was a menacing laugh, made all the worse by the fact that Carey could feel himself trapped by the weight of his own body, unable to move or react. A kick to the ribs made him groan in pain, but that was the only response he could give while semi-unconscious.

Carey was only vaguely aware of what was going on, but he heard distinctly different sets of footprints stomping through the house, not even attempting to be quiet. He phased in and out of consciousness, but came to just enough to know that he should at least pretend that he was out cold, letting them think he wouldn't be a threat.

"This one's half-dead and useless," he heard an unfamiliar voice call out. "Go check the house and see who else you can drag out here." Retreating footsteps thudded across the wood floors, followed by the sounds of different doors opening and closing as a search was underway.

Carey had to will himself to stay silent as gun shots rang out somewhere down the hall, followed by raised voices. Another gun shot sounded, then it was silent. The radio crackled near where Carey had been keeping watch, but there was no voice: Amy's code for something wrong.

Barely able to turn his head for the throbbing pain in his skull, Carey tried to look around the room. He couldn't see anyone, and so was jolted sharply when a hand landed on the back of his neck. "Carey?" Amy whispered in his ear, the fear coming through in her shaky voice. "Can you hear me? Carey!"

He moaned in response, letting her know he was at least alive. He heard her sigh of relief then felt her breath near his ear as she spoke. "Stay put, don't try to get up. I'll be back. I'm going to make sure everyone in the kitchen is okay, then go look for the others."

Everything he felt told him to scream for her to come back, to tell her to stay and not put herself in any danger. Carey winced as he finally rolled over, able to open his eyes for a moment but shutting them again when the ceiling above him continued to spin. When he could finally look up without being flooded with nausea, he forced himself first to his hands and knees, and then to his feet. There was no way he was letting Amy face this alone, not when she'd had to overcome her own fears and lack of confidence.

This was his land, damn it! He was the oldest Carson here now, and he no longer cared that his brother had left home. Carey wasn't going to stand in his brother's shadow, a place that he'd put himself in of his own free will, when there were people here in danger. He staggered to the kitchen, holding on to the nearest furniture as he moved. He was confused by a bloody hand-print on the wall next to the door frame but instead of being sickened when he realized it was his blood, left there by his unsteady hand, he was angry. Rage coursed through him at the people who had invaded his family's happiness and threatened women and a teenage boy.

Carey shoved through the kitchen door and grabbed a wooden chair, knocking it to the floor and stomping on one of its legs to break it off. He picked it up and hefted it before walking through the rest of the house, feeling his way through the dark.

The sound of voices from his father's office stopped him, and Carey immediately crouched down to avoid being seen by anyone who may be keeping watch. He slunk along the floor until he could see around the door frame, looking into the office that was illuminated by his father's desk lamp.

NO! Carey thought. *Not her!*

He watched in horror as Crazy Mack dragged Amy roughly by the arm and threw her onto one of the sofas. He stood over her, blocking Carey's view for a second. The ringing sound of a slap vibrated off the ribs surrounding Carey's heart. That was all he needed to launch himself through the door at Mack, tackling him from the side and landing on top of him with a satisfying crunch.

Carey rained down blow after blow on Mack's face, enjoying the beating in a way he would have never thought possible. He had never struck another human being in his life and never thought he would have needed to.

Now, it took every bit of his strength and self control not to kill him.

"Carey! Stop!" Amy said quietly, evenly, coming up to him and bringing him back to reality with the calmness of her voice. "He's done, Carey!"

Carey stopped his fist in mid-swing, looking around as the room came back into focus. His eyes settled on Amy, and he stared into her large eyes as he worked to bring his breathing back to normal. He looked down at his hands, at the blood that peppered his knuckles, wondering for just a second how it had gotten there. His eyes traveled to where Mack lay only semi-conscious, then back to Amy, pleading with her silently to not think of him as a monster.

"What have I done?" He asked her, the question hanging in the air between them without an answer. "Are you okay?" He finally demanded. She nodded; the effects of the intrusion finally crashing over her until she sat back, trying to control the shaking that came over her violently.

Carey crossed over to her, wiping the offensive blood from his hands on his own clothes before he gathered her in his arms, holding her against him as her nerves recovered from what had happened. She leaned into him and closed her eyes, breathing in his scent and letting it soothe her.

"Are you sure you're okay? I heard shooting earlier," he asked, trying to look her over for any signs of damage.

"Yeah. The sheriff."

"The sheriff shot at you?" Carey demanded, enraged all over again as he continued to look to see if she was okay.

"Well, not exactly," she explained in an oddly detached voice. "He thought he was going to. I fired off those shots and took him down."

"You mean you killed him? Are you sure?"

"Yes. I'm really sure," she answered quietly. "I hated to do it, but when he drew his weapon I knew he meant business. I had to dispatch him before he went looking for the others."

"Anders!" Carey yelled, remembering the others and jumping up from the sofa, pulling Amy by the hand toward the kitchen. They broke through the swinging door into the darkened room and paused to let their eyes adjust until Carey remembered that the power had been restored before Mack and Matthews stormed the house. He flipped on the light switch by the door and froze when he saw the empty kitchen, the cots almost stripped and one or two of them over turned.

"Anders! Where are you?" Carey called out as Amy ran to the back door to see if anyone had left to the porch. A freezer door opened a crack before Anders burst through, dragging the others out of the freezer, wrapped in the thin fabric blankets. Even though the power had been out, the large walk-in freezer had retained most of its chill.

Anders grabbed Carey and hugged him, fighting back tears. "We all went in the freezer when I heard the gun shots," the younger brother explained.

"We sure did," Amanda spoke up, beaming at the boy. "He's a genius. He got us all in there, and even thought to bring the blankets."

Carey looked at Anders with an entirely new respect. This wasn't just the sickly younger brother they'd all looked after growing up. He might not be a ranch hand or know his way around the barn, but Anders was important to the ranch in other ways, ways Carey or the others would never have been able to fill. He ruffled his brother's hair for a second before hugging him close again.

The sound of approaching vehicles made them all freeze. Now that the sheriff was dead and Mack was practically hog-tied and unconscious, there was no way of knowing how many other people were in on his drug business. Amy drew her gun and retrieved Carey's rifle, tossing it to him as he ushered the others back into the freezer, making sure they had their blankets again.

Carey and Amy watched out for each other's backs as they crept toward the front door, dropping down when several pairs of headlights shown through the thinly-curtained front windows. They were at a disadvantage, staring as they were directly into the lights beaming through the remaining glass.

A knock on the door was almost a welcome relief, because Carey decided anyone bent on hurting them probably wouldn't knock first. He approached the door with Amy beside him, her gun pointed in front of her toward the floor. "Who is it?" he called out.

"DEA, responding to a call," the gruff voice called out. Amy shook her head no, warning Carey not to open the door.

"Why would the DEA just happen to show up here?" She whispered tensely. "Something's not adding up."

"That was me," Anders called out from the kitchen door. "I called Dad and had him contact them when I heard you and Amy discussing it. It's okay!"

Carey looked from Anders to Amy for confirmation, but Amy only shrugged before nodding in agreement. She kept her gun ready as Carey opened the door, relieved when he saw the officers and the lead agent's outstretched identification. He showed them in, pointing to the locations of Mack and the sheriff, then ran over and grabbed his younger brother.

"You're pretty much a genius, did you know that?" He asked, rubbing his knuckles lightly on Anders' head. He released a very embarrassed Anders and with his other arm, he pulled Amy to his chest. He kissed the top of her head before thinking better of it and finding her mouth with his own. He left a lingering kiss there as the others politely became very occupied with righting the overturned cots and folding the discarded blankets.

"You need a vacation, Officer McDade," Carey said, still holding her. Amy pressed against him, enjoying the security of Carey's embrace.

"I believe I do. In fact, you practically owe me a vacation. I came out here for a good time with cowboys. And you're the only cowboy I see, so..." She left her sentence hanging as she playfully opened the first button on his shirt, pulling back the fabric and placing her lips against a smooth, undamaged area of his skin.

"So?" Carey teased in a thick voice, trying to keep his wits about him as Amy began working free another button. "Am I hearing you right, that you still want a cowboy vacation? I'll have to get to work on that. How about we head out first thing in the morning after everyone gets back? We can take ourselves a nice, long, *real* cowboy vacation?"

"With the horses? And the sleeping under the stars? And all that good stuff?" She hinted slyly, running her hands up Carey's biceps.

"There will be sleeping at some point," he shot back, playing along.

"I do have a couple of concerns, though," Amy cautioned him, her brow wrinkling slightly.

"Oh, really? And what might those be, Officer?" He asked, eyeing her skeptically as he joined in on her joke.

"For starters, I want a smarter horse this time. It doesn't have to pass an IQ test or anything, but it does need to know how to walk forward without trying to kill me. Backward is still negotiable."

"I think I can arrange that," Carey said with a stern, businesslike expression. "Any other requests? Goose down duvets? Spa robes? Little mints on your pillow, maybe?"

"Nope. I don't need those kinds of things. But I do have a question," she said, stepping closer and peering up at Carey with a serious look on her face.

"What would that be, ma'am?" He replied innocently.

"Do we have to bring the cows along this time?"

Carey threw back his head and laughed before feathering her lips with kisses, spectators be damned. Without breaking their kiss, he bent slightly until his arms were around her waist, then lifted her to his height and walked with her out of the kitchen, through the living room, and out the front door to stand under the stars in front of the house. Amy left her arms wrapped around Carey's neck as he gently set her feet on the ground, their kiss deepening as her hands wound their way into his hair. He pressed her body

116

against his, holding her so close she could feel his heartbeat against her skin.

He finally broke the kiss and lifted her chin gently with his fingertips, looking into her eyes. "What if your vacation didn't end?" He asked nervously. "What if you loved ranch life so much that you stayed?"

"Out here?" She asked, surprised. "A city slicker like me? Please, Texas wouldn't know what to do with a Detroit cop running around all over the place. And what would I do all day without the excitement of the city to keep me busy?"

"Well, we do find ourselves in need of a sheriff lately, and you are the one who first made the connection between the sheriff and Mack, and the drugs. I bet you're just the kind of cop we need." He kissed her deeply again, then said, "And I think you're just the kind of woman I need."

Chapter Sixteen

Miranda stepped down off the front steps of the porch and came over to where Casey leaned against the split rail fence that ran the perimeter of the yard. She ran her hands up his back then wrapped her arms around his waist, leaning her head on the firmness of his shoulder blades. "Are you glad to be home, cowboy?" She asked, letting her fingertips slip between the buttons on his shirt and trace a path over the ridges of his chest.

Casey put his hands on top of hers and turned around, leaning back against the fence and pulling her to him. "I am definitely glad to be home," he promised her, leaning in for a quick kiss. "I have to say, you're a trooper. Not many brides are quite so willing to drop everything on their honeymoons and take off for a cattle drive."

"Are you kidding? If all those selfish brides knew how exciting it is to be surrounded by good-looking, muscular cowboys all day long, there would be a riot at the airport with brides ripping up their tickets to the Caribbean to head out west instead!"

Casey raised one eyebrow at her. "Good looking cowboys? Plural? As in, more than one cowboy was good looking?"

"Well, for starters, there's two of you, but you knew that already!" Miranda nodded, acknowledging that he and Carey were still often mixed up for the other one. "But, don't worry, there's only one cowboy who can get my attention, Mr. Carson."

"Well, *Mrs. Carson*, it's still nice to hear you say it! I mean, do I need to be careful with you around my brother because we're both so handsome? He's invited us to have dinner with him tonight, and I'd hate for all this gorgeousness times two to be more than you can handle."

"Well, that would be a real problem," Miranda admitted playfully. "If your brother's date didn't carry a gun. Trust me, I won't be looking at either of you when she's in the room, just to be on the safe side!" Casey laughed before giving Miranda a lasting kiss that left her nearly breathless. "How long's the ride to the hunting lodge?" She asked, wondering whether they'd take the horses or the truck to have dinner with Carey and Amy, where they were staying on her ranch getaway.

"Only a couple of hours if we take the truck, longer if we take the horses, obviously," he answered, smiling as Miranda clearly tried to process living on property that took hours to cross. "I thought we'd pack some overnight things and camp out tonight. What do you think?"

"You haven't had enough of living 'cattle drive' style, have you?" She teased, already plotting how to get him to at least throw a real mattress in the bed of the truck. "I've had plenty of sleeping on the ground to last me at least a month or two."

"Fine, we'll compromise. You sleep in the truck, I'll take the ground," he offered with a quick kiss, knowing she would never go for it. Miranda was shaking her head before he'd even finished.

"Not a chance, Mr. Carson. You're stuck with me from here on out. The justice of the peace said so!" She beamed proudly as she said those words. Casey leaned closer to give her one of his wonderfully ravaging kisses, the kind she could never imagine growing tired of, but first whispered against her lips.

"I wouldn't have it any other way." He held out his hand to her and they walked inside to gather their things, then headed to the truck. Soon enough, they were bouncing along the same piece of land where Casey first took Miranda to propose to her.

"Do you think this old farm of yours is magical enough to be lucky twice?" She asked Casey, leaning her head on his shoulder as he drove.

"What do you mean?" He asked.

"I mean, I didn't fall in love with the ranch, but I fell in love with you because of the man this ranch helped you become. Do you think it can work its magic on Amy's heart in the same way?"

"I can't say for sure," Carey answered. "You know she's a tough sell. I think she really cares about my brother, but even you can see what a culture shock this has to be. You left a good-sized city to move out here, but she'd be leaving behind her city and her sense of purpose."

Miranda nodded thoughtfully. As much as everyone had tried to welcome Amy and make her feel like she belonged over these past three weeks, there was still something about her that seemed hesitant. On the surface, she seemed to enjoy being a part of the ranch, and it was obviously to anyone with even halfway decent eyesight that she and Carey were falling in love. But there was something else, some force field at work inside her that kept Amy from really being a part of it all.

"Well, Carey did say he had some 'big news' for us but he wouldn't tell me anything else," Casey explained. "Maybe their big news is that Amy's going to stay for good and make an honest woman out of my little brother!"

Miranda sat up suddenly, excited over Casey's announcement. "Really? Big news? You sure he said, 'Big news'? How did he sound when he said it, did he sound like it was important, or did he sound surprised?"

Casey laughed, watching the eager expression on his new wife's face. "Whoa! Slow down there! You're gonna hurt yourself with all that guessing! He just said it in a regular way, nothing fancy.

120

I'm sorry, I didn't know his facial expression was going to be on your exam!" Miranda laughed along, then returned to her position beside Casey, her arm wrapped through his, her head on his shoulder.

When they arrived at Carey and Amy's temporary vacation site, the hunting lodge Carson Hill Ranch rented out each season, they were thrilled to see the couple arm in arm on the front steps, waiting outside once they heard the roar of the oversized truck approaching. Carey and Amy waved them in, both of them smiling broadly.

"Welcome, guys!" Carey called out as he and Amy met them beside the vehicle. "What can I carry?" He followed Casey around to the bed of the truck, retrieving bundles of dinner things and supplies.

Miranda and Amy, meanwhile, linked arms and went into the house, but they were only a few steps away when Miranda had to speak up. "So, I heard you have some big news," she began, before squealing and grabbing Amy's left hand, holding it up to inspect its digits for an engagement ring. Amy looked shocked, then mildly amused at Miranda's implication.

"Now don't you start, either!" Amy began, laughing and hugging her new best friend close. "I've been hearing all the hints I need for right now! No, it's a different big news but you'll have to wait until the boys come in. No sense spilling it and then having to repeat it!"

When all four were inside and had had the chance to catch up on the goings on at the ranch, Carey looked to Amy and gestured for her to begin. "Well, guys, someone over here blabbed that I had some news to share." Miranda practically bounced in her seat while Casey leaned forward expectantly. "So, I'll let you guys be the first to know that I've decided to stay in Hale. The judge has appointed me to be the new sheriff!"

Their faces frozen into forced glad smiles, Miranda and Casey alternated between looking at Carey and Amy, and looking at each other. Was this good news, or not? And what did she mean, staying in Hale? That was almost an hour away!

"Um, that's great, Amy!" Casey began, looking pointedly at Miranda to celebrate. She recovered herself and clapped her hands excitedly—maybe a little too excitedly to be believed—before jumping up and giving Amy a hug. "I mean, that is great, isn't it? This is a good thing?"

"Of course it's a good thing!" Amy said with a laugh. "I think it's going to be just the change of scenery I needed to get back into what I love doing. And with the DEA still uncovering how deep the drug ring in Hale goes, I figure I can also be needed around here."

Carey had been fairly quiet during their congratulations, smiling proudly but not saying much. Casey and Miranda exchanged a worried look, but didn't let their nagging worry for the next Carson brother ruin the evening's mood.

While Miranda and Amy sat on the porch after dinner and enjoyed the pampering of the twins having cooked and now offering to clean up, Casey stole a moment to whisper to his brother. "So, you didn't seem too excited about Amy taking that sheriff position."

"Was it that obvious? Damn, I've been working all day on my excited face," Carey said back snarkily. "I mean, I can't even tell you how glad I am that Amy's staying around here, I just wish it was for a different reason than being the right cop to unearth a drug ring."

"Yeah, I get it," Casey replied. "but are you sure that's all it is, and not the fact that she'll be taking the job all the way over in Hale?"

"Well, there's that, too. But we can always figure that out. It's far, but it's not like it's across the country. It's not even across the county!"

"Then what's the problem? You got her to stay in this part of the country, that was a huge decision right there," Casey explained, trying to be sympathetic while getting his brother to see that a major battle—losing Amy as she returned to life up north—had already been won.

"I just don't like this whole business with Matthews and Crazy Mack, it's just not sitting right with me that these things were happening right next door to us all this time, and we never knew about it." Carey paused his pacing in the small kitchen and leaned back against this kitchen sink, running his hands through his hair. "And now, Amy's going to get tangled up in all of it. I think she was right all along, this goes a lot deeper than just two local boys. I just can't stand the thought of something happening to her, and she's gonna go off and fight the bad guys!" Carey complained quietly, casting nervous glances to the front door to make sure they weren't overheard.

"Dude, it's gonna be okay. If that girl can survive in Detroit, then I don't think Hale, Texas is gonna be too be a leap for her!" Casey didn't know that Amy almost didn't survive Detroit, and that was a huge part of the reason she'd stayed, knowing there wasn't much of a life to go back to in the city.

Carey nodded begrudgingly, admitting there was some truth to what Casey said. "You're right. Deep down, I know it but it's still hard to think about."

Miranda called from the front porch for the brothers to join them, and the four of them sat together and visited under the stars. After their conversation dwindled down to a comfortable, thoughtful silence, Casey spoke.

"Carey, *now* would you please put my wife out of her misery? She's trying really hard to hold it together, but I don't know how much longer she can take it," he asked in an exasperated tone. It was Amy who giggled first, causing Carey to laugh along.

"What are you talking about?" Miranda demanded, pretending to be angry and narrowing her eyes at Casey. She watched the three of them laugh good-naturedly at her expense before nearly losing her patience, making them laugh even louder. "I'm not playing, you guys! Someone tell me what's going on, before I die from the suspense!"

It was Amy who finally ended the torture as she extended her hand to Miranda, waggling the fingers on her left hand and letting the row of diamonds on her now-replaced ring catch the moonlight.

"Carey asked me to marry him, and I said yes!"

The End

Thank you for reading and supporting my book and I hope you enjoyed it.

Searching For Love

CPSIA information can be obtained
at www.ICGtesting.com
Printed in the USA
LVHW052124030520
654917LV00032B/2091